Charles K. True

The Life and Times of Sir Walter Raleigh

pioneer of Anglo-American colonization

Charles K. True

The Life and Times of Sir Walter Raleigh
pioneer of Anglo-American colonization

ISBN/EAN: 9783337392550

Printed in Europe, USA, Canada, Australia, Japan

Cover: Foto ©Andreas Hilbeck / pixelio.de

More available books at **www.hansebooks.com**

THE

LIFE AND TIMES

OF

SIR WALTER RALEIGH,

PIONEER OF
ANGLO-AMERICAN COLONIZATION.

BY

CHARLES K. TRUE, D. D.,

AUTHOR OF "ELEMENTS OF LOGIC," "LIFE OF JOHN WINTHROP," ETC.

CINCINNATI: CURTS & JENNINGS.
NEW YORK: EATON & MAINS.

PREFACE.

THIS book is composed to find a place in Sunday-school libraries, to keep in memory the heroic men who have contributed to lay the foundations of Anglo-Saxon civilization on this Continent, in the hope that it may alternate with, if not substitute, some of the fictitious tales that make up so much of the reading of our young people. It is based upon the most recent and reliable biographies of Raleigh and the histories of his times. I take pleasure in acknowledging my indebtedness to the biographies of Raleigh by Edward Edwards and by Mrs. M. A. Thompson, English writers, and to J. C. Ridpath's "History of the United States."

C. K. T.

Flushing, L. I., N, Y., 1877.

CONTENTS.

ILLUSTRATIONS.

SIR WALTER RALEIGH.

LIFE

OF

SIR WALTER RALEIGH,

Pioneer of Anglo-American Colonization.

———•———

Chapter I.

BIRTH AND EDUCATION.

SIR WALTER RALEIGH was born A. D. 1552, at the Manor Hayes, in the parish of East Badleigh, on the eastern coast of Devonshire, a county distinguished as the birthplace of two other great navigators, Sir Francis Drake and Sir John Hawkins. It was in the reign of the young king, Edward VI, son of Henry VIII and Jane Seymour, whose death at the age of fifteen gave the throne to Mary, the Catholic, daughter of Henry VIII and Catherine. His parents were Protestants, as we know by the following anec-

dotes, well worth noting, as revealing the character of the times:

A few years before Walter was born a revolt
against the government of the papists, called the
"Rising of the West," took place. It commenced
on Whitsunday, 1549, at the Church of Sampford
Courtenay, about twenty miles from Hayes, and
spread all over Devon and Cornwall. While riding toward Exeter, Walter Raleigh, Senior, overtook an old woman going to the Church of Clyst
St. Mary. He amused himself by asking her,
"What is the good of your beads?" and told her
of the new laws against superstitious practices.
She was made so angry by his banter that, when
she got to the church, she rushed in and cried
out, "Unless they would quit their beads and
holy water, the gentlemen would burn their houses
over their heads!" The Congregation thereupon
swarmed out of the church "like a sort of
wasps;" and a party of them overtook Raleigh,
and obliged him to flee into a chapel on the road-
side, where he was protected for the time; but
farther on he was overhauled and captured by a

party of rioters, and imprisoned in the tower of a church at Saint Sidwell's, in the suburbs of Exeter. The rebels besieged Exeter; but, in a bloody battle at Clyst Heath, Lord Grey defeated them with great slaughter.   In the morning after the battle Mr. Raleigh was set at liberty by the victors.

In the next reign the work of suppressing Protestantism was carried on with vigor by Queen Mary, and many good people were martyred for their religion.   Among them was one uneducated but strong-minded and pious woman, named Agnes Prest, whose trial so excited the sympathies of young Walter's mother that she made her a visit of condolence in prison.   The poor woman revealed the special cause of her imprisonment while repeating to Mrs. Raleigh her creed; for when she came to the words, *"He ascended,"* she stopped and remarked upon the folly of looking for the body of Christ in any earthly temple; and declared the papal usage of the sacrament was making an idol of the wafer, and not a proper remembrance of Christ's passion.   Mrs. Raleigh was surprised at her intelligence, and said to

the family that she was convinced that "God
was with her." "I was not able to answer her—
I who could read, and she can not!"

We know nothing more of the mother of
Walter, except that she was the widow of Otho
Gilbert, a man of wealth, and became the third
wife of Mr. Raleigh. By him she became the
mother of three children, Carew, Walter, and
Margaret. By her first husband she had three
sons, Humphrey, John, and Adrian Gilbert, all of
whom attained distinction, especially the eldest.
We shall find him, in the course of our narrative,
the Sir Humphrey Gilbert exploring the "North-
west Passage."

The rustic house in which Walter was born
still remains, with various alterations and additions, amidst rural scenes that have scarcely
changed since. "It is of the plainest sort of
Tudor architecture, with three gables, heavily
mullioned windows, a thatched roof, and somewhat picturesque porch." It was within a pleasant
walk of the coast, which made him conversant
with sailors who had visited all parts of the globe,

and it was in the neighborhood of manufactories established by emigrants from Flanders; and on every side were exhibitions of trade and enterprise and thrift, the early types of that marvelous industry and art which has made England the foremost nation of the world.

The name of the family was spelled in every possible way—Rale, Rawley, Rawleigh, Ralegh, and Raleigh. We retain the latter because it is so spelled in our American geographies, though Sir Walter's autographs show that he spelled it Ralegh, without the *i*. It is curious to observe how utterly erratic was the spelling of even learned persons of those days, having no standard, and showing no reluctance to employ double letters for single, spelling the same word differently in the same paragraph, and all such vagaries.

All we know of Walter's early education is that he was entered as a commoner at Oxford University in Christ Church College, and also in Oriel College, probably for the chance of a fellowship in one or the other of the colleges. He was a student three years, and was distinguished for his attainments in philosophy and oratory; but he did not remain long enough to graduate.

At the University he made the acquaintance of Francis Bacon, who formed a high opinion of his talents. Bacon tells this story of him: "Whilst Raleigh was a scholar at Oxford, there was a cowardly fellow, who happened to be a very good archer; but, having been grossly insulted by another, he bemoaned himself to Raleigh, and asked his advice what he should do to repair the wrong that had been offered him. 'Why, challenge him,' answered Raleigh, 'to a match of shooting!'" Very witty, and wise too, compared with the barbarous fashion of dueling.

Chapter II.

RALEIGH ENLISTS IN THE CIVIL WARS OF FRANCE—THE HUGUENOTS.

IN the Autumn of 1569 he leaves college, and engages as a volunteer under his cousin, Henry Champernoun, to fight on the side of the Huguenots against the King of France. He was probably at the battle of Jarnac, and certainly in that of Moncontour, for in his "History of the World" he extols the masterly ability of Count Ludovic, brother of the Prince of Orange, in conducting the retreat of the Protestant army after being defeated in battle, thereby saving it from utter demoralization and destruction: "of which," he records, "myself was an eye-witness, and was one of those that had come to thank him for it."

These facts connect our hero with a portion of history that will never cease to be of tragic interest.

The Protestants of France were named Huguenots as a name of contempt. It is derived from
a compound German word meaning *confederates*.
They were mostly Calvinists, and, at the time in
question, were found in every part of France,
and numbered two million. They had endured
every sort of persecution; many had been condemned by the *Chambre Ardente* to be burnt for
heresy, and their estates were confiscated. At
length, in 1560, being secretly encouraged by
Condé, a prince of the blood royal, a conspiracy
was formed to resist by arms the tyranny of the
government. The plot was discovered, and cost
the lives of about one thousand two hundred
persons.

On the accession of Charles IX to the throne
of France, being advised by the queen mother,
Catherine, he granted toleration and many privileges to the persecuted sect. This awakened the
jealousy of the Catholics, and especially of the
Duke of Guise, the chief minister of State. A
civil war was imminent. A number of Huguenots, engaged in worship in a barn, were insulted

by the servants of the Duke as he was passing
that way, and in the *mélée* which followed the
Duke was wounded in the face by a stone. Seeing this, his attendants became furious, and killed
a number of the Huguenots. The reports of this
affray went abroad in an exaggerated form, and
in a short space the whole country was in a blaze
of civil war.

The first battle was fought at Dreux, and the
Huguenots were defeated, and their commander,
Condé, was taken prisoner.

The next year the Duke of Guise, while at
the siege of Orleans, was stabbed by an assassin.
On his dying bed he exhorted the queen mother,
who had unbounded influence at court, to make
peace with the Huguenots. She complied with
his request, and favorable terms of pacification
were granted; but in a few years after, the war
broke out afresh. In the first battle, the leader
of the Huguenots, the Constable Montmorenci,
was killed. The next great battle was fought at
Jarnac, March 13, 1569, and the Prince Condé
was obliged to surrender. Being wounded, he

was placed by a tree, when an officer of the enemy came behind him, and in a dastardly manner shot him dead.

Queen Elizabeth, who was now on the throne of England, did not formally engage on the side of the Protestants; but it had all her sympathies, and she winked at the unauthorized participation of her subjects in the war. Men, ships, provisions, and money were freely contributed, which so offended the government of France that it was on the point of declaring war against England.

The religious conflict went on in France, and finally culminated in the massacre of St. Bartholomew's Day. The Queen Mother Catherine, now become ferocious, conceived the diabolical purpose of murdering at one fell stroke all the hated Huguenots in the kingdom. It required all her art to inveigle the young king into her scheme; but at last he yielded. The night of the 24th of August, 1572, was set for the execution of the plot. The great bell of the palace was rung, and the Swiss guards of the king led

the way for the whole military to enact the horrid
scene.   The Duke of Guise rushed with a band
of soldiers to the residence of the Admiral Coligny, the aged and venerable leader of the Huguenots, and surprised him in bed.   As one of
the assassins approached him with a drawn sword,
he said to him, "Young man, you ought to reverence these gray hairs.   But do your work; my
life can be shortened but a little."   His body was
thrown out of the window.   It was taken to
Rome, and hung on a gibbet by the feet.   In
this manner every house where Huguenots lived
was broken into, and its inmates were put to
death, without respect to age or sex.   And the
same scenes were enacted in every province of
the realm.   Seventy thousand persons, it is reckoned, perished in that dreadful night.   The young
king murdered his own peace, for he never knew
rest to his conscience from that hour.   His Protestant nurse, whose life he had spared, was with
him at his dying hour.   Hearing him groaning,
she went to his bed, and opened the curtain, and
asked what distressed him.   "Alas, nurse!" he

cried. "What blood! what murder! Ah, I have followed wicked counsel! O my God, forgive me! Have mercy upon me if thou wilt!"

Raleigh was in France at this time, and until 1576. How he escaped, the massacre, and of what he was doing, we have no account. His own silence on the subject is accounted for by the fact that the English allies of the Huguenots had no authority from their own government for enlisting in the civil wars of France, and they fought with the assurance that, if taken prisoners, they were liable to be hung. The persecution of the Hugueuots, of which we have a glimpse at this point of history, went on for a century, until the land was cleared of them by death and emigration. More than two millions of the best inhabitants of France fled to Switzerland, Germany, England, and America, carrying with them art, wealth, and the principles of the Reformation.

Chapter III.

DISCOVERY AND COLONIZATION OF AMERICA—RALEIGH'S FIRST ADVENTURES.

COMING from the civil wars of France, we trace Raleigh to his native land, planning with his renowned step-brother Humphrey Gilbert to make discoveries of the north-west passage.

As early as A. D. 986, an Icelander named Herjalfson, on a voyage to Greenland, was overtaken by a storm, and driven to a land that was so different from Greenland that they knew it was another country. From his stories about it on his return it is conjectured to have been Labrador or Newfoundland.

This awakened the spirit of discovery in others, and an expedition was fitted out under Captain Lief Erickson, in A. D. 1001. He discovered and explored the coast of Labrador. Thence he sailed southward as far as Massachusetts, and the

next year went on to Rhode Island, and round to
the mouth of the Hudson, River.   The same
year, 1002, his brother Thorwald took the same
route as far as Fall River, Massachusetts, where
he died.   In 1005, another brother, Thorstein,
came to Massachusetts.   In 1007, Thorfinn Karl-
sefne, a noted navigator, took one hundred and
fifty men, and made explorations along the coast
as far as Virginia.   They gave the country the
name of Vinland.   Small colonies were planted
by Norwegian and Icelandic adventurers in Newfoundland and Nova Scotia.   But all these attempts were ephemeral, and nothing came of
them.   In after years vessels from Norway visited
these coasts.   They were supposed to be a con-
tinuation of Greenland, and no idea of a new
continent discovered ever came to Europe until
after Columbus had made his discoveries.

His idea was that, the earth being a globe, a
passage could be made to the Indies by proceeding westward.   As early as 1356, in the first
English book ever printed, Sir John Mandeville
expressed this conviction, derived from his own

observation of the stars in traveling northward and southward.   But it was reserved to Columbus to reduce the speculation to experiment.   In the evening of the 11th of October, 1492, after seventy days' sailing, he saw a light moving on the horizon which betokened land, and when the morning dawned he heard the cry of "land!" from Rodrigo Triana, and in a little while he stepped ashore at the Isle of San Salvador, with the flag of Castile in his hand, and followed by his rejoicing crew.   In this voyage he discovered Conception, Cuba, and Hayti, and having built a fort out of the timber of one of his little ships, the *Santa Maria*, he returned to electrify the Old World with the news of his success.   On his second voyage he discovered Jamaica and Porto Rico, and on the third he discovered the South American Continent near the Orinoco River.

In 1499 Amerigo Vespucci discovered the South American coast, and again in 1501 he explored it, and published the fact that it was not India, but another continent.

In 1510, a Spanish colony was planted on the

Isthmus of Darien. The governor, Vasco Nunez de Balboa, crossed the Isthmus, and first saw the Pacific Ocean, and pompously took possession of it in the name of the King of Spain.

Florida was discovered in 1512 by Juan Ponce de Leon, who made a landing near St. Augustine. On a second voyage to this region he was shot by an arrow from the Indians, who resisted his landing, and he withdrew, to die of his wound in Cuba.

In the year 1517 Yucatan and the Bay of Campeachy were discovered by Fernandez de Cordova, who met the same fate at the hands of the natives. Two years afterward Cortez began the invasion and conquest of Mexico.

In 1519 Ferdinand Magellan, a Portuguese captain, set out from Seville, under the patronage of the King of Spain, to discover a south-west passage to India; and, after spending several months in Brazil, the next Spring he passed down to the straits which now bear his name, and penetrated into the Pacific. Then, proceeding westward, he reached the Ladrones, and after that the Philippine Islands, where he lost his life in a battle with the natives. The fleet went on to the Moluccas.. There one vessel took in a cargo of spices, and leaving the rest, as too much strained to pursue the voyage, passed round the Cape of Good Hope, and reached Spain in safety, with the announcement that the world had been circumnavigated.

In 1520 the coast of South Carolina was visited by the infamous Lucas Vasquez de Ayllon, who, being driven by a storm, put into the St. Helena Sound and the Cambahee River. The natives came on board to trade, and while the decks were crowded with them he set sail, and carried them off and made slaves of them. One of his ships went to the bottom in a storm, and all on board perished. In a few years he returned to the same spot. One of his ships ran aground, when the Indians made an assault upon it and killed many of the crew, and compelled De Ayllon to escape as best he could.

In 1526 Charles V granted to Pamphila de Narvaez the territory from Cape Sable to the River of Palms, and in 1528, with a force of three hundred men, he entered Tampa Bay and landed to explore the country, and took possession. But after incredible hardship the whole of this force perished, except four men, who came out of their wandering on the Pacific Coast, at what is now the village of San Miguel.

The year 1539 saw a fleet of ten vessels, under Ferdinand de Soto, enter Tampa Bay, commissioned to explore the country. Our limits will not allow us to follow the marvelous fortunes of this company, as they traversed the regions east and west of the Mississippi as far as the borders of the State of Missouri. Disappointed in his pursuit of El Dorado, and overcome by fatigue, De Soto fell a prey to a malignant fever, and was buried in the Mississippi River.

It was not till 1568 that the attempt to colonize Florida was renewed, and then it was for the diabolical purpose of dispersing a Huguenot colony that had formed a residence on the St. John's River. Philip II gave the command of the expedition to Pedro Melender. Having laid the foundations of St. Augustine, the first town planted in the present territory of the United States, he started on his murderous enterprise, and surprised the colony of Protestants, and butchered them, men, women, and children, to the number of two hundred. Seven hundred seamen were in the neighborhood, having escaped from their wrecked vessels, which had gone down the river expecting to meet the hostile forces by the way of the sea. These were captured and marched to St. Augustine, and there were slaughtered without mercy. The leader of the Huguenot colony, Laudonniere, with a few men, escaped to the coast, and were rescued by the two vessels that had escaped the storm which sent the rest to their destruction. How mysterious the ways of Providence, that he should allow the elements to conspire with the wickedness of man to extinguish the light of the Reformation on these shores! It was his will that Protestant colonies should be planted further northward.

In 1501 a Portuguese captain named Cortereal explored the coast of Maine, and carried off fifty natives, and sold them as slaves in Europe. The next year he went on the same nefarious expedition, but was never heard of afterward.

France sent her fishermen to the Banks of Newfoundland in 1504; and 1524 an expedition was fitted out by Francis I to discover a northwest passage. John Verrazzani, a Florentine, commanded a fleet of four vessels when they started, but three of them were disabled by a tempest, and he proceeded with but a solitary ship. He first touched the coast in the neighborhood of Wilmington, North Carolina; thence he passed along to New Jersey and to New York Harbor; thence to Newport and the coast of Massachusetts; thence to Nova Scotia and Newfoundland. He gave the name of New France to these countries. In 1534 James Cartier came with two ships to Newfoundland, and then, seeking the northwest passage, he discovered the Gulf and River St. Lawrence. The report of this awakened the deepest interest in France, and he was commissioned to plant a colony in this region. He penetrated the river in boats as far as Montreal, and wintered there four years afterward. Cartier was associated with Francis of La Roque, Lord of Roberval, to lead another colony to the St. Lawrence. Finding the people uninclined to enlist, the Government adopted the expedient of giving liberty to the prisoners who would volunteer to embark for America. With this strange company they entered the St. Lawrence in 1541, and selected the present Quebec as the site of the settlement, and built a fort. But though this colony was re-enforced the next year with a fresh supply of the same sort of persons, the whole enterprise failed and came to naught.

This ended French colonization for fifty years, as attempted by the Government.

In 1562 the Huguenot Admiral Coligny obtained from Charles IX the privilege of sending forth a colony of the persecuted Protestants, under Captain John Ribault. They first touched at Florida, and then came to Port Royal, where they erected a fort, and gave to it the name of Carolina, in honor of the king. There he left twenty-four men; but not being able to re-enforce them, on account of the troubles of the times, they became discouraged, and constructed a vessel and left for France. The next attempt was made in the neighborhood of St. Augustine; but it was destroyed by Melendez. Vengeance was taken for this slaughter by Dominic de Gourges, who came with three ships and surprised three of the Spanish forts, and hanged the captives on trees, with the inscription over them, "Not Spaniards but murderers."

In 1598 the Marquis de la Roche planted a small colony of forty released criminals on Sable Island, but they escaped back to France by ships passing the coast.

In 1605 De Monts planted in Nova Scotia the first permanent French colony in North America, and gave the country the name of Acadia.

In 1608 Champlain made a second voyage to the St. Lawrence, and settled a colony at Quebec. The following year he discovered the noble lake to which his name is given.

Glance now at English adventurers.

The first discovery of the real Continent of North America was made in 1496 by John Cabot, who, in the employ of the English Government, bore the flag of England to the coast of Labrador full fourteen months beore Columbus saw the coast of Guiana. He took the country to be the kingdom of the Cham of Tartary. By the side of the English flag he set up the flag of his native land, the Republic of Venice!

In 1498 his son, Sebastian Cabot, visited the country discovered by his father, and explored the whole coast as far southward as Cape Hatteras.

In 1576 Martin Frobisher, searching for the north-west passage, discovered the strait called by his name, and afterward also Hudson's Strait, in latitude 63° 8'. The next year he returned to the same region, but did not dare to go so far north on account of the icebergs; and the year following he renewed the attempt, and passed into Hudson's Strait.

Sir Francis Drake in 1577 passed through the Straits of Magellan into the Pacific Ocean, and ascended as far as Oregon in search of the long-desired passage, and gave the name of New Albion to all this coast.

We come now to the part which our hero,
Walter Raleigh, had in the colonization of North
America by Englishmen.   His step-brother, Sir
Humphrey Gilbert, obtained from Queen Elizabeth a patent to take possession of any six hundred square miles of territory not yet occupied on
the coast of North America.

A large company were associated in this enterprise, and ample preparations were made to put
to sea, when the English Court interposed on account of objections made by the King of Spain,
who absurdly claimed the whole of America as his
dominion by right of previous discovery and oc-
cupation!   However, the two brothers, disregard-
ing this injunction, set sail with two vessels; but
they were met at sea by Spanish men-of-war, and
after an engagement in which they suffered defeat
with the loss of many men, they were obliged to
put back.   Five years afterward the attempt was
renewed under better auspices.   To this we shall
return, after we have followed our hero to another
and far different engagement in Ireland.

Chapter IV.

CIVIL WARS IN IRELAND.

THE Irish people, being mostly adherents of the Church of Rome, and of an aspiring and turbulent disposition, have never been contented under the rule of Protestant England. The entire reign of Elizabeth was marked by tragic scenes of rebellion, riot, and civil war. In 1570, Philip II instigated a plot to revolutionize Ireland, and to place the natural son of Pope Gregory XIII on an independent throne. This movement was thwarted; but in a few years it was revived under the leadership of the Earl of Desmond. The insurrection took formidable shape in Munster. At Smerwich, in Kerry, an invading party of Spaniards and Italians landed under the command of San Joseph, and constructed a fort, which they called "Del Oro."

Walter Raleigh enlisted for the suppression

of this rebellion, and was actively engaged, we know not to what extent, under the command of Thomas, Earl of Ormond, and Governor of Munster. In 1580, we find him one of a commission to try James, the brother of the Earl of Desmond. The case was a clear one, and the execution of this distinguished rebel had a great influence to discourage the insurrection. At Rakele an encampment was vacated by the English forces, and was immediately taken possession of by the Irish. This was anticipated by Raleigh, and an ambush was laid for them, and they were taken prisoners. One of the prisoners had a bundle of withes on his shoulder, and being asked what he was going to do with them, he replied: "To hang up the English churls with!" "Is it so?" said Raleigh; "they shall now serve for an Irish kerne." And he ordered the man to be strangled with his own willows. He has been censured for this act; but he justified himself by necessity of striking terror into the minds of the rebels.

A certain Lord Barey, in the county of Cork,

was suspected of abetting the rebellion, and Raleigh, at his own request, was ordered to surprise him in his castle at Barey Court. His coming was anticipated, and an ambush was laid for him at a ford near Cork. With great presence of mind he collected around him his little band, and made a dash upon the thick ranks of the troops opposing his march, and fought his way through them. In the fight, a follower named Henry Moyle, to whom he was attached, twice foundered in the bog, and was twice rescued by Raleigh at the hazard of his own life. He was at another moment struck from his horse, and stood face to face with twenty men, with nothing but his pistol and quarter-staff to defend himself. But he escaped, and so did every man in his escort. He lost nothing but his horse, and gained the reputation of a great fighter.

It was deemed of greatest importance to destroy the garrison of Del Oro, at Smerwich, by which Spanish vessels were supplying the rebellion with all kinds of stores and munitions of war. The Deputy Lord Grey commanded the land

forces in person, and Admiral Sir Wm. Winter the
fleet sent to besiege the fort. The attack was resisted three days, when Captains Raleigh and
Mackworth penetrated the fort, and demanded
unconditional surrender. A white flag was held
out; but Lord Grey would listen to nothing but
absolute submission. "The enemy," writes the
Deputy in his dispatches to the government,
"begged for a surcease of arms. I definitely
answered I would not grant it. Either presently he must take my offer, or else return, and
I would fall to my business. He then embraced
my knees, simply putting himself to my mercy;
only he prayed that for this night he might abide
in the fort, and that in the morning all should be
put into my hands. I asked for hostages for the
performances. . . . Morning came; I presented my companies in battle before the fort.
. . . I sent straight certain gentlemen to see
weapons and ammunition laid down. Then I
put in certain bands, who straightway fell to execution. There were six hundred slain. Those I
gave life unto, I have bestowed upon the cap-

tains and gentlemen, whose service both well deserved."

This cruel slaughter was disgraceful even for
those times; but it was apologized for by the
poet Spenser and others as a justifiable treatment
of the foreign "brigands," many of whom were
criminals released from Italian prisons by the
Pope, and sent to maintain insurrection and rebellion in a distant land.

One notable adventure of Raleigh was his
seizure of Lord Roche at his estate in Prathy,
about twenty miles from Cork. This nobleman
was suspected of secretly aiding the rebellion,
and Raleigh deemed it important to take this
prop from the rebels, and offered to undertake
his capture, and bring him and his family to
Cork. Some of the rebels got wind of this, and
a force of eight hundred men, under Fitz-Ed-
monds, were thrown in Raleigh's path; but he
was too quick for them, and by a night's march
got by the place for the ambuscade before they
had reached it. At Prathy he found five hundred
men in arms awaiting him; but he managed with

his small escort to amuse them, while he, with a handful of men, made his way to the castle, followed by another small band. Arrived at the gates of the castle, the guards objected to his entrance with more than two attendants; but Raleigh managed deftly to get his six soldiers inside, and the others coming up had the same success. Lord Roche, finding an armed force within his gates, made the best of the circumstances; protested his loyalty to the queen, and ordered a table to be spread for the entertainment of his unexpected guests! Raleigh lost no time in making known his purpose to take him away to Cork and exhibited the warrant for his arrest. Nothing could be done but for him and his family to get ready for a night journey to Cork. This was accomplished over unfrequented routes, at considerable peril, and with the loss of one soldier's life, who fell from the rocks, and the wounding by falls of several others. They avoided, however, the ambuscades on the direct road, and at dawn Raleigh presented his prisoners to Lord Ormond. Upon examination, Lord

Roche was honorably acquitted, and was never after suspected of complicity with the rebellion. Indeed, he took an active part in support of the queen's authority, and three of his sons fell in battle fighting for the government.

Upon the recall of Ormond as Deputy, a joint commission was given to Raleigh and two other gentlemen to act as governors of Ireland. He established his headquarters at Cork. In furious conflicts with rebel forces he displayed much skill and bravery. At Clove he had a horse shot under him, and would have lost his life but for the attachment and bravery of one of his followers, Nicholas Wright. In 1582 he was relieved from his command, and returned to England, having the satisfaction of seeing the rebellion quelled.

Chapter V.

RALEIGH AT THE COURT OF ELIZABETH — ESSEX — LADY
ARABELLA STUART—SIR PHILIP SIDNEY—SPENSER.

SOON after Raleigh's appearance at Court, a
question concerning the management of
affairs in Ireland by Lord Grey was argued before
the Council Board, and Raleigh, who took ground
against the Earl, was heard by the Council in the
presence of the queen.   His penetrating, piquant,
and splendid delivery won her admiration, and
from this time, Sir Robert Naunton remarks, "she
took him for a kind of oracle," and loved to hear
him debate any case he might have occasion to
present to her.   On his part, he was bent on
securing the personal affection of Elizabeth.   It
is related that he met her one day on the marshy
shore at Greenwich, and, to save her from wet-
ting her feet, threw down his gorgeous velvet
cloak for a carpet.   He addressed to her some

adulatory poetry; and on a window of the palace, where it was sure to meet her eye, he scratched, with a diamond ring:

"Fain would I climb, but that I fear to fall."

Seeing it, she wrote under it:

"If thy heart fail thee, climb not at all."

Elizabeth was about forty years of age, ten years the senior of Raleigh. She could not, for state reasons, allow her affections to be engrossed by any of her admirers, but was nevertheless susceptible of the romantic sentiment of love. Nor could Raleigh have aspired to any thing more— but so much he meant to have. He was well calculated to interest any lady. To his fame as a soldier and scholar he added the charm of a countenance expressive of intelligence and resolution, a tall and well-proportioned form, manners graceful in the extreme, and a copious and ready wit in conversation. He prided himself on his costly and elegant dress, after the showy fashion of the day. In one of several portraits extant, his array is a white satin pinked vest with close

sleeves, a brown doublet, flowered and embroi-
dered with pearls, a pearl-embroidered belt, a
dagger with a jeweled pommel, a black feather in
his hat, contrasted with a ruby and pearl drop,
white satin trunk hose, and buff-colored shoes,
tied with white ribbons. His silver armor was
preserved in the Tower, as a curiosity. On one
occasion his shoes were adorned with jewels
computed to be worth upward of six thousand
six hundred gold pieces! Such a display would
excite disgust in this day; but it passed for good
taste in the court of the queen. She too was
fond of rich and showy attire. In person she was
described by Sir Robert Naunton as "tall, of hair
and complexion fair; and therewithal well favored, but high-nosed; of limbs and features
neat; of a stately and majestic comportment."
She was specially proud of her delicate hands.
"She pulled off her gloves more than a hundred
times," said a contemporary of an audience he
had with her, "to display her hands, which were
indeed very beautiful and very white."

Notwithstanding her serious attention to public

business, Elizabeth was fond of amusements, and many were the pageants, plays, masques, and tournaments which were exhibited in her court, and marked her costly visits to the seats of her favorite noblemen. In all these pastimes Raleigh bore his part, and every day ingratiated himself in the affections of the queen, as the celebrated Leicester had done at an early period of her life. This favoritism was a matter of public gossip, and was severely criticised. A foreign embassador, writing home, calls her Cleopatra; and even a popular actor, Taylor, ventured to point to Raleigh while repeating in the part he was acting the words, "See how the knave commands the queen!" The queen resented it, and banished him from the court. Spenser confessed to Raleigh that he meant him and Elizabeth in the Timias and Belphœbe of the "Faerie Queene."

A letter written to Sir Robert Cecil, when Raleigh was by the queen's order a prisoner in the Tower, as a punishment for his intrigue and marriage with Elizabeth Throckmorton, displays only the courtly style of adulation, rather than real affection: "My heart was never broken till that day that I hear the queen goes away so far off, whom I have followed so many years with so great love and desire in so many journeys, and am now left behind here in a dark prison all alone. While she was yet near at hand, that I might hear of her once in two or three days, my sorrows were the less; but even now my heart is cast into the depths of all misery. I, that was wont to behold her riding like Alexander, hunting like Diana, walking like Venus, the gentle wind blowing her fair hair about her pure cheeks like a nymph. Sometimes setting in the shade like a goddess; sometimes singing like an angel; sometimes playing like Orpheus. · Behold the sorrows of this world!" It is clear enough that Elizabeth's heart was more touched than Raleigh's, and that it was her jealous, disappointed love which punished him so severely.

But we anticipate our story. At present Raleigh is in high favor, and his influence is sought even by distinguished noblemen. He is appointed lord Warden of Stannaries (that is, tin mines),

lieutenant of the county of Cornwall, vice-admiral
of Cornwall and Devon, and finally captain of the
Queen's Guard, a troop chiefly distinguished by
personal figure and splendid uniform.

He was sent in the suite of the Earl of Leicester
to Antwerp to honor the inauguration of Francis
of Valois.   He obtained grants of license to
export broadcloths, and the "farm of wines,"
that is, authority to grant licenses to traders, and
to regulate prices.   This, however, did not on
the whole prove so very profitable to him, while
it involved him in some lawsuits, and especially
in a disagreeable controversy with the University
of Cambridge, which claimed this privilege within
its own precincts.   The greatest gift of the queen
to her favorite was the estates of Anthon Babing-
ton, who, in 1586, was convicted of conspiring to
assassinate her.   This man was the head of an
ancient family in Northumberland, and had large
possessions there and in Derbyshire.   He was
educated by the Jesuits, and led a wild and dis-
sipated life.   He was taught by his priest, one
Ballard, that it would be no crime to kill an ex-

communicated princess, but doing God service. The motive was to make room for Mary, Queen of Scots, who was the next heir to the throne, and a Roman Catholic. During his confinement in prison he made an overture through friends, or arranged to do it, to get Raleigh to intercede for him with the queen, and offered to pay him a thousand pounds if he could procure his pardon. But there is no evidence that Raleigh gave the least heed to his solicitation even if it reached him. The queen's grant not only made Raleigh rich in lands and manors and tenements, forfeited to the crown with all the rents, profits, and revenues thereof, but no acknowledgment and no fee was required of him in receiving the great seal to his grant.

About this time there came a rival in the favor of the queen in the person of Robert Devereux, the young Earl of Essex. He was that smart boy, who, when eleven years of age, turned away from the queen when she offered to kiss him. And he was now not even twenty years of age, but ripe beyond his years, and possessed of very many graces and accomplishments.   He was put upon this career, it has been said, by the Earl of Leicester, Elizabeth's old favorite, out of jealousy of the growing favoritism of Raleigh.   Any how, the queen took this young and handsome nobleman at once to her good graces, and he became very intimate with her.   "When she is abroad," said a spectator of court life, "nobody is near her but my Lord of Essex; and at night my Lord is at cards, or one game or another with her till the birds sing in the morning."

Very soon he became arrogant, and resented the partiality of the queen for the splendid captain of her guards.   He went so far as to write to a friend that he said to her, "I was loth to be near her, when I knew my affections so much thrown down, and such a wretch as Raleigh highly esteemed of her!"   Fine language, if indeed he ever said it, to a queen by an upstart of twenty years of age!

Another person, the Lady Arabella Stuart, whose tragic fate resembles so much that of Raleigh, was about this time introduced to him.

She was the granddaughter of Henry VII, and
cousin of James I, and so after him, if he had
no children, she would be heir to the throne of
England.   A plot of some nobles, abetted by the
Pope, who imagined she was inclined to Roman-
ism, to set aside James in her favor, was the
cause of her ruin, though she was wholly innocent
of the affair.   She was now but eleven years of
age, very beautiful and accomplished, and it was
whispered in Raleigh's ear that it was a pity she
was not older, to which he replied, "It would
be a very happy thing."   Edward Edwards mentions this piece of gossip, and adds, "When the
same names were brought together on the latest
occasion of all, Arabella lay beneath her shroud
in the prison, which to her had but shortened
life, and embittered while degrading it.   Raleigh
was beneath the same gloomy roof, and above
his head the fatal clouds were beginning to gather.
But in his case a long imprisonment had given
birth to an immortal book.   Save for the twelve
years in the tower, English literature would have
lacked one of its glories."   But we shall come

to that fall soon enough; at present life was wearing all the bright hues of joy and promise.

Among the favorites of Elizabeth should be mentioned Sir Philip Sidney, especially as he was a friend of Raleigh, and in literary genius and knightly valor much resembled him. He was born in 1554, the son of Sir Henry Sidney, an officer in government of Queen Mary. He was educated at the universities of Oxford and Cambridge, and after his graduation traveled several years on the continent. Elizabeth, on his return home, took him into her service, and sent him on an embassy to Germany. His sensitive nature was so ruffled by a quarrel with the Earl of Oxford, that he abruptly left the court, and retired to the seat of the Earl of Pembroke, who had married his sister. There he employed himself in the completion of a romance, which he entitled, in honor of his sister, "The Countess of Pembroke's Arcadia"—a work which for the time was a superior model of English prose, and contributed to fix the English tongue. He meditated an expedition with Sir Francis Drake against

4

the Spanish settlements in America, but was per-
emptorily forbidden by the queen to engage in it.
In 1585, he was mentioned as a candidate for the
crown of Poland; but this, too, Elizabeth objected
to, not wishing, she said, "to lose the jewel of
the times." He was subsequently made governor
of Flushing, a town in the Netherlands, ceded to
the English for services against the Spaniards.
As general of the horse he joined his uncle, the
Earl of Leicester, who commanded the army of
the English assisting the Dutch against Philip of
Spain. In 1586 he achieved the capture of the
town of Oxel as captain of a detachment of English troops. The same year, in a skirmish with
the enemy at Zutphen, he received a wound in
the thigh which proved mortal. As he lay upon
the field, a cup of water was brought to him;
and as he was putting it to his lips, a wounded
soldier was carried by who looked so wistfully to
the cup that Sir Philip ordered his attendants to
give it to him, saying to the soldier, "Thy necessity is greater than mine." His death spread
gloom over the court of England, and Raleigh lost

a friend whose loss could not be made up to him.
He was but thirty-two years of age at his death.
His other writings extant are the "Defense of
Poesy," "Astrophel and Stella," and "Songs and
Sonnets."

The best of his sonnets, as I think, is the
following :

"O happy Thames, that didst my Stella bear !
  I saw thee, with full many a smiling line
Upon thy cheerful face, joy's livery wear,
  While these fair planets on thy stream did shine.
The boat for joy could not to dance forbear,
  While wanton winds, with beauties so divine
Ravished, staid not, till in her golden hair
  They did themselves,O sweetest prison, twine,
And fain those Æol's youth there would their stay
  Have made ; but forced by nature still to fly,
First did with puffing kiss those locks display,
  She, so dishevel'd, blushed. From window I,
With sight thereof, cried out, oh fair disgrace !
Let honor's self to thee grant highest place."

Another literary friend of Raleigh was Edmund
Spenser, the first great poet of England after
Chaucer. He was born in London, at East
Smithfield, near the Tower, in 1553, and gradu-
ated at Pembroke College, Cambridge, 1569. He

was employed in the capacity of secretary by
Lord Grey, while Lord Deputy to Ireland; and
in 1586 he received from the queen a grant of a
portion of the Earl of Desmond's forfeited lands.
The condition was that he should reside in Ireland, and accordingly he occupied the old Kilcolman Castle. Here he wrote the "Faerie Queene,"
which, more than any thing else, has immortalized
him. The peculiar stanza employed was his own
invention, and now bears his name. Lord Byron
has employed it in his "Childe Harold," with the
greatest success. Sir Walter Raleigh visited him
when he had finished three cantos, and the
friends spent a delightful hour together in reading
and commenting upon the poem. He has celebrated both Elizabeth and Raleigh in his verse,
giving the latter the style of "Shepherd of the
Ocean." In his forty-first year he married the
lady whom he celebrates under the name of
Elizabeth in that magnificent epithalamium, which
is deemed the greatest of the kind in English
verse. The rebellion of Tyrone, in 1598, drove
Spenser and his family from Kilcolman, and so

hurried was their flight that they left behind their infant child. The mob set fire to the house, and the babe perished in the flames, with all the contents of the house which they did not choose to pillage. The heart-broken poet escaped to London, where, overcome with misfortune, he soon after died. He was buried in the tomb of Chaucer, in Westminster Abbey. His wife found refuge with her two sons, living in another part of Ireland; and after the rebellion was suppressed she returned to Kilcolman. In 1641 another outbreak sent a second wave of desolation over the place. She fled, to return no more; and the place fell out of the possession of the family until Cromwell the Protector restored it. In now belongs to the Earl of Clancarty.

It was the influence of Raleigh that induced Spenser to bring out the three cantos of the "Faerie Queene" before more were written. These were published in 1596, but only fragments have been found of what would have been the concluding six, had the troubles of the times not driven him from home and ended his life.

Chapter VI.

RALEIGH ATTEMPTS TO COLONIZE VIRGINIA.

THE bad success of the first effort for colo-
nizing America of Sir Humphrey Gilbert,
with whom Raleigh was a partner, in 1579, as
related in Chapter IV, did not discourage the
devoted brothers. Raleigh exerted all his influence with Queen Elizabeth in favor of renewing
the enterprise. In 1583 five ships were fitted out
at great expense, and set sail for Plymouth on the
11th of June. The queen told Sir Humphrey
that "she wished as great good-hap and safety to
his ship as if herself were there in person." She
gave him as a present "an anchor guided by a
lady," which he was to wear on his breast, and
asked him to leave with her his picture as a keep-
sake. Raleigh did not himself embark, but contributed two thousand pounds to equip one of the
ships, which, after him, was named *The Ark Raleigh.*

It unfortunately happened to this ship that an infection broke out among the crew soon after she left port, and she was obliged to put back. Sir Humphrey saw them putting back, and supposed that they had treacherously deserted him, but he went directly on with the remaining four ships. They discovered Newfoundland early in August, and Sir Humphrey took ceremonial possession of it in the name of his sovereign. The insane passion for gold and silver and precious stones reigned in the breasts of all the early discoverers of America; and in this instance the sailors, having discovered mica in a hill, took it for silver, and went to work to load one of the ships with the precious metal, regardless of the order of the commander and of the purpose of the expedition to settle the country. One of the ships was condemned as useless, and with the three that were left Sir Humphrey at length got away, and proceeded down the coast. Off Massachusetts a storm overtook them, and the ship laden with supposed treasure went down, carrying with her a hundred men. This determined Gilbert to steer

for home.   But he was destined never to reach
England.   A storm soon ingulfed the vessel in
which he sailed.   At midnight the two ships
came within hailing distance, and Gilbert shouted
to his comrades in peril, "Be of good cheer, my
friends; we are as near to heaven by sea as by
land!"   The other ship brought to England the
sad tale of the shipwreck of her consort and the
loss of all on board.

Six months after this the undaunted Raleigh
obtained a new charter, by which he was author-
ized to take possession of and colonize such
countries as were not already possessed by other
Christian States; and to repel all intruders who
might approach nearer than two hundred leagues,
and to exercise all civil and military rule in this
settlement for six years thereafter, provided the
laws enacted be conformed as near as may be to
the statutes of England, and "not oppose the
Christian faith."

Under this charter Raleigh dispatched two
ships, commanded by Philip Amidas and Arthur
Barlow.   In July they came in sight of the coast

of North Carolina, and landed at the island of
Roanoke. "There lieth," says William Strachey,
an historian of those times, "along the coast a
tract of islands two hundred miles in length, and
between the islands two or three entrances.
When they were entered between them, there
appeared an inclosed sea, in which were one
hundred islands of diverse bigness, whereof
Roanoke is fifteen or sixteen miles long, a pleasant and fertile ground, full of cedars, sassafras,
currants, flax, vines, deer, conies, hares, and the
tree that beareth the rind of black cinnamon."
There the company were entertained by the
Indian queen, and welcomed to the country.

But these captains had no genius for colonization, and after exploring the coasts of Pamlico and
Albemarle Sounds, and getting such an impression
of the country as would make a basis for glowing
rhetoric on their return to England, they came
away, bringing with them some specimens of
skins, "a bracelet of pearls as big as pears," and
two of the native Indians.

Raleigh seems not to have resented this

fruitless expedition. He was delighted with the account of the beauty and richness of the country, and sought and obtained permission to honor the queen by naming it "Virginia." On a new seal of his arms he had his name engraved in Latin as "Lord and Governor of Virginia."

The idea now of colonization took possession of the popular mind in lieu of the impractical notion of finding a north-west passage, and Raleigh got the Parliament, in December of that year, 1584, to enlarge his charter. And now large numbers, including young men from the nobility, enlist in a new expedition. Sir Ralph Lane is engaged by Raleigh to be governor of the colony, and Sir Richard Greenville to command the fleet consisting of seven ships. There were no less than one hundred householders on board, and such notable men as Thomas Hariot, the mathematician, and Captain Thomas Cavendish were associated with them; but no females were in the company—a fatal lack in view of permanent colonization. When near the coast off Cape Fear, they encountered a fearful storm; but they weath-

ered it, and arrived safely at Roanoke on the
26th of June. With a portion of the emigrants,
consisting of one hundred and ten persons, Lane
commenced the work of forming a settlement,
while Greenville made explorations along the
coast, in the course of which, in the piratical
spirit of the times, he seized a Spanish treasure
ship. But he made no attempts to form another
settlement, and returned to England with his
prize.

Lane- very soon came into collision with the
natives of the land. He set fire to an Indian
town on the island simply to retaliate an act of
theft committed by some of the inhabitants, and
by such measures set the whole native population
against him. Soon after he was lured into the
depths of the mainland by reports of gold mines,
and came near being captured by the Indians.
He retaliated by entrapping the Indian king Win-
gina and other chiefs, and putting them to death.
Of course, the country was roused against them,
and he got ready to quit the country. Sir Francis
Drake in this emergency happened to be passing

by on his return from the Pacific coast, and took the colonists back to England, where they arrived July 27, 1586. Soon after a supply ship arrived from Sir Walter Raleigh, and two weeks after that Sir Richard Greenville himself arrived with a fleet of three ships, laden with stores of all kinds, and re-enforcements of men. He was surprised and amazed to find the colony gone; but he left fifteen men to still hold possession, and returned to England. Was ever a scheme of colonization so foolishly managed? The settlement had not lasted two years.

The next year, 1587, saw a new experiment commenced by Raleigh under better auspices. Captain John White was appointed governor, with a charter of municipal government, and he embarked with one hundred and fifty householders. The government was styled, "The Governor and Assistants of the City of Raleigh in Virginia." They avoided the dangers of Capes Fear and Hatteras, and landed at Roanoke in the month of July. To their sorrow, they found no traces of the fifteen colonists; but they commenced their foundations of the new city at the north end of the same island.

The old story of war with the natives has to be told, and the usual results followed. Raleigh counseled a pacific policy, and he adopted an expedient, which, whatever effect it might have on aristocratic Englishmen, was powerless for good in Virginia. He got Manito, an Indian chief, made a peer of the realm, with the title of Lord of Roanoke. The colonists now began to begin to be in dread of want, and they urged Governor White to return to England for supplies. He left them, and they perished at the hands of the aborigines, it is supposed, for no account has ever been given of their fate. It is worth mentioning that the first child of English parents born in America was born August 18th. She was named Virginia Dale. This was the end of Sir Walter's costly efforts to colonize Virginia. He strove to reach the colony by two supply ships; but they were seized by Spanish cruisers, and when White returned in 1590, under the direction of a London society, to whom Raleigh sold out

his proprietary rights, he found nothing but deso
lation where the city of Raleigh was to have been
founded.   The expense to Sir Walter of all these
nine expeditions was not less, it is reckoned, than
two hundred thousand dollars.   But his name is
worthy of everlasting honor in America, and the
city of Raleigh, in North Carolina, though on
another site, will ever be his monument to posterity of his unparalleled devotion to American
colonization.

Elizabeth was now so involved in the war with
Spain that she could give no aid to colonization.
The terrible Armada was coming, and the fate of
the nation was at stake.   Nothing more was done
for Virginia during her reign.   It remained for
Captain John Smith to take up the work where
Raleigh left it, and after great hardships and re-
verses to get the first plant of English civilization
to take root at Jamestown, on James River, named
in honor of Elizabeth's successor on the throne of
England.   The words of Raleigh came true, "I
shall yet live to see it an English nation."

One reminiscence of this ill-fated colony is the

tobacco plant.   When Lane returned with Drake he brought specimens of it, and contributed to introduce the custom of using it in England, as it was already more or less prevalent in Spain, Portugal and France.   Sir Walter Raleigh was fond of it, and one day he was amusing himself with "drinking" the smoke (that is, taking it into his mouth, and letting it come out of his nose and ears), when his servant came in, and, thinking that his master was on fire, he seized a bucket of water, and dashed it on his head. Elizabeth did not favor its use by her example. One day she made a wager with Raleigh that he could not ascertain the weight of the smoke.   He won the bet by weighing first the tobacco used, and then weighing the ashes.   The difference was the answer.   The queen laughed, and paid the wager, saying "she had heard of those who turned their gold into smoke, but had never before seen the man who could turn smoke into gold."

Chapter VII.

RALEIGH'S RELATION TO IRELAND—POTATOES INTRODUCED
INTO IRELAND—WAR WITH SPAIN—THE
ARMADA—REPRISALS.

IF tobacco was a damage to the nation, another plant, the gift of Virginia, was one of
the greatest blessings. It was on his estate in
Munster Sir Walter was the first to plant the po-
tato in Ireland. We have seen how, after the
suppression of the Irish rebellion, large landed
estates were bestowed upon Raleigh. To all the
concessions the crown attached the requisition
that the owner should re-people the estates with
loyal people from England. He went to work
with zeal, and from Devonshire and Somerset-
shire brought industrious tenants, and soon gained
the reputation of having the best ordered and
best cultivated lands in Ireland. But property
obtained by confiscation was destined to bring

trouble, and he had his full share. It would be tedious to detail these troubles; suffice it to say that he grew weary of them, and finally sold out nearly all his interests to Richard Boyle, afterward Earl of Cork. There remained to him only one castle, which for her jointure was occupied by the old Countess of Desmond. This lady lived to be an hundred and forty years of age, and saw nine successive reigns, from Edward IV to James I.

Raleigh was severe in his views of policy in the government of the Irish. He believed in showing no quarter to rebels. It is related that a Captain Leigh killed a noted insurgent named Feogh Machugh, in fair fight, and cut off his head, and sent it as a present to the queen. It was sent back again, by the same messenger, to be thrown among the carcasses of other rebels; and the error was pardoned in view of the intent. Raleigh advised that the court should not deal harshly with such cases. The rebels deserved to have a price put upon their heads, seeing they "sought the lives of anointed princes."

5

At this time, 1587, Drake was upon the sea, destroying the commerce of Spain. More than one hundred vessels of all kinds were sunk by him in a single year. He wrote to Lord Bur-leigh that "there never was heard of or known so great preparations as the King of Spain hath and daily maketh ready for the invasion of Eng-land." Pope Sextus V had formed a powerful league for the suppression of heresy, and the chief in this conspiracy was Philip of Spain. He had a large army in the Netherlands under the greatest captain of the age, and he was preparing the greatest fleet that ever before was known for the invasion of England. The queen was fully apprised of her danger, and put forth all her masculine energies to arm the nation for defense, by land forces and fortifications and by ships of war. Raleigh took an active part in these prepa-rations. As governor of Devon and Cornwall, he organized the militia, strengthened the fortifica-tions of the Isle of Portland, and contributed largely to the arming of ships, which he regarded as the best defense that could be made.

The commander of the English fleet was Lord Howard, of Eppingham, who, though a Roman Catholic, had the confidence of the whole nation as a truly loyal man and an able admiral, descended from a line of naval heroes. A spy at Madrid gave notice of the sailing of the Armada in the month of May, 1588. This took the ministry by surprise, for they had sent word to Howard to return to harbor with his ships, to save expense. He was of a different opinion, and protested that he would rather have the expense of the ships charged to his account. Soon the report of the approach of the formidable fleet off the coast showed the correctness of his information and judgment. It consisted of a hundred and forty sail of all kinds, from galleys to the largest frames that ever floated, carrying in all twenty-six hundred and fifty guns, eight thousand sailors, twenty thousand soldiers, and two thousand volunteers of distinguished rank.

As they entered the British Channel, Howard went out to engage them with only six ships, but was soon joined by others, to the number of

thirty.   The object of the Spaniards was to reach
Calais to make communication with the Duke of
Parma, and to take aboard his army, and cross
over to the English coast and effect a landing.
They were pursued and annoyed by the fast-
sailing English ships, and lost their principal ship
and many galleons.   In the night, after coming
to anchor, eight fire-ships were sent amongst
them, which so frightened them that they weighed
anchor and moved off.   In their disorder they
were furiously assailed by the English ships, and
numbers of them sunk or captured.   At length
the Spanish commander signaled orders to return
by the way of the North Sea.   So poorly were
the English ships supplied with ammunition, that
now they felt that they were unable to complete
the victory by further pursuit.   At this juncture a
terrible storm arose, and the flying ships were
wrecked at sea, or driven upon the coasts of
Scotland and Ireland and Norway, and not half
of the "Invincible Armada" escaped to tell the
fate of the expedition.

Sir Walter did not get ready to join the English

fleet until the second day of the engagement, but he was one of the last to give up the pursuit and leave to nature the finishing of the terrible retribution on the enemy.

The thousands that were wrecked on the coast of Scotland and Ireland were taken captive, and sent to England to await the judgment of the queen. Magnanimously she refused to order them to be put to death, and sent them home to Spain, to tell the tragic story in the ears of their countrymen.

In token of the Divine Providence which had so signally defeated the diabolical purpose of the Spaniards, Queen Elizabeth had medals struck with the motto, "*Afflavit Deus et dissipantur.*" (God breathed on them, and they are scattered.)

Edward Edwards relates that Lord Burleigh received a letter from Rome stating that Cardinal Allen was overheard saying that the King of Spain had given "great charge to the Duke of Modena, and to all the captains, that they should in no wise harm the person of the queen; but should as speedily as might be give order for the con-

veyance of her person to Rome, to the purpose
that His Holiness the Pope should dispose thereof
in such sort as it should please him!" So man
proposes, but how differently God disposes!

Had the invasion of England succeeded, the
history of Europe and America would have been
far otherwise than we now read, and this country
would be a Spanish colony.

The defeat of the Armada left the English
cruisers at liberty to rove the seas, and to make
reprisals on Spanish commerce. Sir Walter Raleigh had three ships, the *Crown*, the *Garland*,
and the *Revenge*, and did much damage to the
enemy; and not always, it is to be feared, with
such regard to the rights of neutrals as is required by international law. "They are Spaniards in disguise," was his answer to a complaint
of this kind, made against one of his captains for
seizing a ship flying Dutch colors.

Sir Walter took part also in the expedition
commanded by Drake and Norris, to aid Don
Antonio, King of Portugal, to recover his crown,
usurped by Philip II. This enterprise failed;

but they succeeded in making a prize of a large
fleet of sixty ships, laden with supplies for another Armada which was to be fitted out against
England.

Chapter VIII.

VISIT TO SPENSER — PANAMA SCHEME — FAVORS TOLERA-
TION — UDALL — THE BROWNISTS — THE JESUITS — RA-
LEIGH'S MARRIAGE — DISGRACE AT COURT AND IM-
PRISONMENT.

FOR some unexplained cause, Raleigh about this time lost the favor of Elizabeth, and took occasion to visit Ireland, and to spend some time with his friend, the poet Spenser.

On his return to court, he took advantage of a temporary suspension of hostilities with Spain to plan a scheme for divesting that nation of some of her American dominions by the conquest of Panama and other regions of America. For this purpose he fitted out, at great expense, thirteen vessels. The queen added two ships of war, and made Raleigh admiral of the expedition.

He was vexatiously delayed by contrary winds months after preparations were made; and, to crown all, when he had fairly got started he was overtaken by an order from the queen to resign the command to Sir Martin Frobisher, and to return to the court. What was precisely the queen's motive for this is not known, but it was pretended that she wished his services at court.

Sir Walter made no haste to obey, but kept on with his fleet until he had made such investigations of the designs and warlike preparations of Spain as to induce him to change the whole plan of his adventure. He gave up his designs on Panama, and divided his fleet into two parts, one for cruising after the rich India caracks that were expected, and the other to hover about the coast of Spain, to engage the attention of the Spanish home fleet, and keep them from coming out to protect the caracks.

After taking a valuable prize of another sort, they fell in with the caracks, and one of them, the *Madre de Dios*, was captured. Another was set on fire by her own crew. The prize was taken to Dartmouth. It proved to be possessed of wealth beyond all calculation, and produced the greatest excitement all over England, every body trying to make capital out of it. The queen managed to get the lion's share, while ˆRaleigh had less than his due. In Spain the utmost indignation was felt at an order now given by Philip II to all his adherents to blow up any ship rather than to let it be taken by the English cruisers.

It is a pleasure at this time to contemplate Raleigh as a courtier favoring toleration in religion at home. Rev. John Udall, of the established Church, had become a non-conformist, and written in favor of Reform in ecclesiastical polity. He was a man of learning and eloquence. The first Hebrew grammar in English was written by him. His principal work on Church reform was entitled, "The Demonstration of Discipline which Christ hath Presented in his Word for the Government of the Church in all Times and Places until the World's end." For publishing this work he was absurdly charged with libel on the queen's majesty, and was brought to trial in fetters. He was condemned on written depositions against him, no personal testimony being admitted, and no written defense allowed to him.   He was sent to prison, and remained a year before he received sentence of death.   Raleigh's attention was turned to this unhappy case, and he took an earnest interest in his behalf.   He got word to Udall to write through him a letter to the queen protesting his loyalty as a subject of the realm.   He did so, praying that his punishment might be commuted to banishment.   A reprieve was granted, and it was proposed to send him to Guinea on condition that he should be kept there until his sentence was revoked by the queen.   Udall objected to this condition, and while the subject was yet pending, he was taken ill, and died in prison.

Raleigh in the same spirit united with Essex to resist the expatriation of the Brownists.   Robert Brown was a minister of the Church of England; but his studies in theology produced in his ardent mind a deep conviction that the polity of the established Church was anti-christian.   He preached on this subject in Norwich in 1581, and converted a number to his views, and for this was arraigned before the ecclesiastical commissioners, who con-

demned him partly for his heresies and partly
for his rude behavior, and sent him to prison.
Obtaining release in a short time, he went with
certain of his disciples to Zealand. There he
wrote a book entitled, "A Treatise of Reformation without Tarrying for any Man." In 1585
he was back again in England, and went on
with his work of reformation until he was ex-
communicated by the Bishop of Peterborough.
He was subsequently made obsequious to the rule
of the Church, and accepted a living in North-
hamptonshire, of which it is said "he received
the emoluments without discharging the duties."
His opinions, however discussed, made him unpopular; but his violence of manner intensified
his troubles, and made him a martyr. He boasted
that he had been in thirty-two prisons, and finally,
in 1630, he died in Northampton jail, where he
was imprisoned for "assaulting a constable and
insulting a magistrate." The views of this ex-
traordinary man were shared by many better
people than himself, and a sect was established
in the north of England called Brownists, among

whom was the Rev. John Robinson, and the glorious band, who fled first to Holland and afterward to Plymouth in Massachusetts—the pilgrims of the *Mayflower*—the beginning of the noble Church of American Congregationalists.

A law was propounded in Parliament against the Brownists and other schismatics, which drew out the eloquent opposition of Raleigh. The law specified that "any person above sixteen years of age who refused, during the space of a month, to attend public worship, should be committed to prison; and if persisting for three months in such determination be *banished the realm under pain of death if detected in returning.*" Against this law Raleigh, though sharing the popular prejudice against heretics, protested as unjust, cruel, and impolitic. "In my conceit," he said, "the Brownists are worthy to be rooted out of a commonwealth; but what danger may grow to ourselves if this law passed were fit to considered? For it is to be feared that men not guilty will be included in it; and that law is hard that taketh life and sendeth into banishment, when man's intentions shall be judged by a jury, **and they** shall be judges of what another means. But a law which is against a fact is just; and punish the fact as severely as you will. If two or three thousand Brownists meet at the sea, at whose charge shall they be transported? and where shall they be sent? I am sorry for it, but I am afraid that there are near twenty thousand of them in England; and when they are gone, who shall maintain their wives and children." This argument shows the dawn of the true idea of religious toleration, which Roger Williams first fully developed and crystallized into public law, and which is now the glory of both England and America. He prevailed so far as to have the bill committed for revision to a committee, of which he was appointed a member.

The modifications of this law which Raleigh secured were as favorable to Roman Catholics as to Protestant dissenters; but on account of his opposition to the Jesuits and their seminaries he excited the wrath of one Father Parsons, who was chief penitentiary of this order in Rome, and was sent to England by the pope to establish his order there, with a view to the displacing the Protestant succession to the crown. This man got up a cry of atheism against Raleigh, and a charge of planning a school of infidelity in which the Bible was a subject of ridicule. His real offense was, advising Queen Elizabeth in council to issue a proclamation against the Jesuitical establishment, a measure which has saved England from their machinations, and which has been again and again imitated by the governments of Catholic nations.

While the pope held a temporal scepter, and assumed to be chief of the kings of the earth, the Jesuits were not to be regarded as a religious sect merely, but as principally a political society, scheming for the ascendancy of the papal power over all nations. At this day, though the pope has lost his crown, and is nothing more than chief bishop of Roman Catholics, yet he still holds his claim to the triple crown, and his emissaries are striving to restore him to his lost position. It is right, therefore, that they should be treated differently from strictly religious sectarians.

We come now to a scene of tragic romance in the life of Raleigh, which was to affect his whole subsequent life. He excites the deepest displeasure of the queen by a secret marriage with Eliza-beth Throckmorton, one of the ladies of the bed chamber. Why he should conceal his courtship and marriage from the queen is not known, though the most recent and authentic biographies ascribe it to her jealousy of all rivals to the affection she claimed of her favorites. Lord Essex, two years before, had the same experience by his secret marriage with Frances Walsingham, the widow of Sir Philip Sidney.

Elizabeth was the daughter of Sir Nicholas Throckmorton, a man of superior mind and culture, descended from an ancient and honorable family. From the pictures of her, which have been copied from originals, she appears to have possessed surpassing beauty of face and form, and her subsequent life shows her possessed of mental and moral traits befitting the wife of such a man as Sir Walter Raleigh. She was eighteen years his junior, and she survived to mourn his tragic death nearly as many years.

The queen was piqued by this clandestine alliance, and immediately dismissed her maid of honor from her court, and deprived Sir Walter of his office as gentleman of the privy chamber, and ordered his imprisonment in the Tower. Some other complaint, probably in reference to his seizure of prizes, may have been connected with this harsh treatment; but it is all a matter of inference and conjecture, as no account of it appears in State records.

Spenser's "Faerie Queene" is supposed to refer to this affair, and to make disappointed love the real cause of Elizabeth's excessive displeasure. Timias attends Belphœbe, and attracts her love. One day a young lady, Amoret, is seized in a forest by a wild man of the woods, and Timias comes to her rescue. A battle ensues of doubtful issue, until Belphœbe is seen by the monster to approach, and he flees, to encounter a sharp arrow from her bow, and dies. Upon coming to

6

the scene of the conflict she finds Timias fondly
striving to restore Amoret from a swoon into
which she was fallen.

> "There she found him, by that new lovely mate,
>   Who lay the whiles in swoon full sadly set,
>   From her fair eyes wiping the dewy wet,
> Which softly 'stilled : and kissing them atween,
>   And handling soft the hurts which she did get ;
> For of that carle she sorely bruised had been ;
>   Which, when she saw with sudden glancing eye,
> Her noble heart with sight thereof was filled
> With deep disdain and great indignity,
> That in her wrath she thought them both t' have thrilled
> With that self arrow which the carle had killed,
>   Yet held her wrathful hand from vengeance sore ;
> But drawing nigh, ere he her well beheld,
> 'Is this thy faith ?' she said, and said no more,
> But turned her face and fled away for evermore."

It is certain that Raleigh had more or less
personal attachment to the queen, and deeply
regretted the loss of her friendship.

An amusing story is told of an outburst of his
emotions on being informed that the queen was
about coming to visit Sir George Carew, keeper
of the Tower. Seeing the royal procession approaching in gay barges, he became almost frantic

with passion to get out of prison, and to get into a boat in disguise, and see the queen. Sir George resisted his importunity, and swords were drawn, which might have proved fatal to one or both of them, had not Sir Arthur Gorges, who happened to be present, interfered. In doing it, Sir Arthur received a severe cut on his knuckles, which arrested their attention, and "they stayed the brawl," he says, "to see my bloody fingers. I was ready to break with laughing to see the two scramble and brawl like madmen, until I saw the iron walking, and then I did my best to appease the fury. As yet I can not reconcile them by any persuasion, for Sir Walter swears that he shall hate him while he lives for so restraining him from the sight of his mistress; for that he knows not (as he said) whether he shall see her again when she is gone the progress." This absurd adulation shows how Raleigh wrought on the affections of a maiden queen, and made it an unpardonable offense to love and marry another.

His imprisonment was not solitary. He had the company of his young and beautiful wife, whose attachment to him was unbroken through all the vicissitudes of his eventful life, and his many friends were allowed to visit him without reserve. He was called out for a time to attend to the apportionment of the spoils found in the *Madre de Dios*. His influence with the sailors was unbounded, and there was a great huzzaing when he came among them. The queen exceeded every body in her rapacity, and Raleigh, captive as he was, protested against it. His own expense for the expedition was thirty-four thousand pounds, and the share allowed him by the government was only thirty-six thousand pounds. The envy of Lord Burghley was partly the cause of this injustice. This was the man that Spenser describes in the "Ruins of Time"—

> "O grief of griefs! O gall of the hearts!
> To see that virtue should despised be
> Of him that first was raised for virtuous parts,
> And now, broad spreading like an aged tree,
> Lets none shoot up that nigh him planted be."

After Raleigh's release from the Tower, we find him cultivating gardens at his place in Sherborne, Dorsetshire.

Chapter IX.

EXPEDITIONS TO GUIANA.

GUIANA, as now known, is that portion of South America lying on the north-east slope of the continent, south of the Orinoco River, and extending as far as the Sierra Acarai, and not to the Amazon River, as formerly marked in the geographies. The largest part of it is possessed by the British, Dutch, and French. English Guiana has three sections—Essequibo, Demerara, and Berbice. The region on the coast is level, and in the interior mountainous. The valleys are exceedingly fertile, and the hills are full of minerals of various kinds; but it has no gold or silver mines of any value. It abounds with beasts and birds and fishes and reptiles similar to most tropical regions. The descendants of the aborigines are yet numerous, and occupy chiefly the remote interior. There is also a race of negroes, de-

scended from fugitive slaves, who formerly gave
the Dutch settlement much trouble by their in-
cursions.

Guiana, in the days of Queen Elizabeth, was
reported to be the realm of the golden city of
El Dorado. This was the name first given to an
imaginary king, who was said to powder himself
with gold dust, and then go and wash in the
rivers, and so scatter the precious spangles all
over the sands. The wildest ideas of gold mines
and banks of gold obtained among European adventurers, which lured them from home, and left
them to disappointment. Sir Walter Raleigh was
affected by these dreams. He wrote a history of
Guiana, in which he says: "Many years since he
had knowledge by relation of that mighty, rich,
and beautiful empire of Guiana, and of that great
and golden city which the Spaniards call El
Dorado and the natives Manoa." He first sent
forth, in 1594, two pioneers, Whiddon and Parker, who brought back word that there was an
El Dorado there, but it was six hundred miles into
the interior. They were specially instructed to

explore the Orinoco River; but they acquired but little information in regard to it. However, encouraged and assisted by Sir Robert Cecil and Lord Howard, Sir Walter went forward in his preparation for a voyage of discovery and perhaps settlement. He fitted out a fleet of five vessels, with all sorts of provisions, barges, and boats for ascending the streams, instruments for mining, and arms for defense. He left Plymouth on the 9th of February, 1595, and in about six or seven weeks he reached the Island of Trinidad off the north coast of South America. On his way he captured a Spanish vessel laden with fire arms, from which he exacted a ransom, and also a Flemish ship, from which he took twenty butts of wine.

The Spanish governor of Trinidad was Antonio de Berreo. This man had maltreated Whiddon, and imprisoned some of his crew, and he was guilty of cruel treatment of the natives. Sir Walter directly made an attack upon the town of St. Joseph, and captured it, and took Berreo prisoner. He found five Indian caciques or chiefs

bound to a single chair, on whom Berreo had in-
flicted inquisitorial tortures. He liberated them,
and treated them with the utmost kindness, as
he did all the natives who came on board his
ships. Berreo, who had made a voyage up the
Orinoco, he spared, and made him useful as an
informer and guide in his expedition. This man
had married a daughter of a previous discoverer
on condition that he should pursue the enterprise,
and he related to Raleigh all that he knew about
the country of Guiana, and much probably that
he did not know. Among other marvels he said
that the natives presented him "with ten images
of fine gold, among divers other plates and crois-
sants, which were so curiously wrought, as he
had not seen the like either in Italy, Spain, or
the Low Countries. And he was resolved that
when they came to the hands of the Spanish king,
to whom he had sent them by his camp-master,
they would appear very admirable, especially
being wrought by such a nation as had no iron
instruments nor any of those helps which our
goldsmiths have to work withal." Berreo had

already sent his lieutenant, Domingo de Vera, to Spain to interest the king in behalf of another exploration and conquest of Guiana. This man told stories about the country and the natives of the most mythical and extravagant character, which have been absurdly accredited to Sir Walter Raleigh, because he recorded them as he heard them in his "History of Guiana." De Vera said the men of that country "had the points of their shoulders higher than the crowns of their heads. They had many eagles of gold hanging on their breasts, and pearls in their ears, and when they danced were all covered with gold." In one province, he affirms, there were "so many Indians as would shadow the sun, and so much gold that all yonder plain will not contain it. They take of said gold in dust, and anoint themselves all over with it to make a braver show, and to the end that gold may cover them, they anoint their bodies with stamped herbs of a glutinous substance." These tales awakened a great enthusiasm of colonization in Spain, and full two thousand persons, including monks and priests,

embarked with De Vera on five ships to take
possession of the real El Dorado. This expedition was on its way while De Berreo was talking
with Sir Walter; and, though he kept assuring him
that the country was full of riches, he nevertheless tried to persuade him that it was too hazard-
ous for the English to attempt its possession.
Among other things of interest related by De
Berreo was that one Martinez, who was put
ashore and deserted by his comrades for neglect
of duty, was picked up by the Indians, and was
actually carried to Manoa, the capital of El Dorado. He was blindfolded when approaching it,
and was kept from seeing any of the surrounding
country; but he was permitted to see the city
when inside of it, and was brought, after travers-
ing the city nearly two days, to the palace of the
emperor.

Nothing daunted, Sir Walter left his ships at
Los Gallos, having put a hundred persons in five
small barges, with a month's provisions and ammunition, and crossed the bay or gulf of Paria
to the mouth of the river. They had a young

Indian for a pilot; but when they got into the river, they found such a multitude of branches that it seemed a perfect "labyrinth" of rivers and islands, and they would have hopelessly lost their way, had they not come upon a canoe with three Indians, one of whom they found to be an experienced pilot. Their voyage was full of difficulty and perils. Twice the largest of the barges run aground, and they were advised by their pilot to leave it, and use only the smaller boats. Doing this, and passing up a narrow stream, they emerged into an open country twenty miles in length, beautifully diversified, and looking like a cultivated land. But after rowing with great toil against the current hundreds of miles, they seemed no nearer the fabled city. They took plenty of game to supply them with meat, but the bread began to be exhausted. At length this demand was met by meeting several canoes of Indians called Arroacas, who supplied them with excellent bread, and also furnished another pilot. The characteristic sudden flooding of the rivers surprised and alarmed them, and having discov-

ered, as they thought, several gold mines which
might be worked with profit, they would have
ended their voyage, had they not a higher end in
view than to find gold.   This object was to survey the country, and mark it for an English colony.   The voyage was pursued as far as the
mouth of the River Caroni, and near the Island
of Tortola.   There he was visited by swarms of
the Indians, who had heard of the difference between Englishmen and Spaniards, and of the kind
treatment of the natives by Sir Walter.   Friendly
trades were made, of fruits and victuals of various
kinds, for such trinkets as were valuable in the
eyes of savages.   Sir Walter entertained the old
chief of this region, Topiawari, with tales of
England, and especially of the wonderful ruler,
Queen Elizabeth; and he seems to be impressed
with the good sense and information possessed by
the aged monarch of the woods.

Had Sir Walter accompanied in person the
various expeditions by which he sought in vain
to colonize Virginia, I can not help thinking, a
different fate would have attended them.   The

one great mistake of American colonization has been cruelty to the aborigines.

While halting his company at the mouth of the Caroni, he sent off parties to hunt for minerals, while he, with a few attendants, went by land to view the falls. The ascent of the river by boats was found impossible on account of the impetuosity of the current. "When we ran to the tops of the first hills of the plains adjoining the river," he writes, "we beheld this wonderful rush of water which ran down the Caroli [now spelled Caroni], and might from that mountain see the river, how it ran in those parts above twenty miles off; and there appeared some ten or twelve other falls in sight, every one as high over the other as a church-tower; which fell with that fury that the rebound of the waters made it seem as if it had been covered over with a great shower of rain; and in some places we took it, at the first, for a smoke that had risen over some great town."

The explorers for gold had no instruments but their daggers to dig into the mines; but they brought back some samples, which were pronounced by assayers in London to be indicative of valuable placers.

They were now ready to return to their ships. Bidding adieu to their new friends, with a promise to return some day, they launched upon the descending current, and made such rapid progress that in a few days they came to the mouth of the river.

At one place they delayed their homeward voyage, and made a visit to a town called Winecoposa. There they found the people celebrating a feast at the house of their chief, and "all as drunk as beggars;" but they were welcomed to partake of their viands and liquor. Withdrawing to their boats, the people came to them from all parts of the country with abundant supplies of fowls and other provisions, including "a delicate wine of pinao."

As they approached the mouth of the Orinoco it was greatly swollen, and rough with surges. A storm set in, and they took shelter under the land with the small boats; but the galley was not so conveniently harbored, and came near sinking, with all on board.   Leaving it to come after, Sir Walter set out, as soon as the storm lulled a little, in his barge, and made for Trinidad and his ships at Curiapan.   Great was their joy when they saw them at anchor where they had left them.   The galley, with the other-boats, coming, in a few days they set sail for England, and arrived there some time in August, 1595.

A narrative of this voyage was published by Raleigh, entitled "The Discovery of Guiana," which, with some colorings and exaggerations of fancy, has been verified by subsequent explorations.   In this he mentions that the old chieftain, Topiawari, urged him to come again, and advised him in that case to make a league with those tribes at variance with the tribes of Inga, otherwise he might share the fate of a former expedition of De Berreo, whose followers were flanked by those border Indians, and three hundred of them killed.   "The borderers, setting the long dry grass on fire, so smothered them as they had no breath to fight, nor could discern their enemies for the great smoke." Two of his company were left with Topiawari by their request, Francis Sparrey, a trader, and Hugh Goodwin, a youth who was ambitious to learn the language of the natives. Sparrey was exhorted by Raleigh to find the great city of Manoa; but he fell into the hands of the Spaniards, and was sent to Spain, whence he escaped to England.

In his second expedition to Guiana Sir Walter found Goodwin at Caliana, in 1617, and obtained from him "a great store of bread." He had been so long in the Indian country that he had almost lost his native language. What became of him afterward is not quite certain, but Oldys reported that "he was devoured by a tiger." On his part Topiawari gave his only son to Raleigh, who took him with him to England.

Raleigh had meditated a visit to his colony in Virginia on his homeward voyage, but the tempestuous weather prevented the execution of his design. Having commission from Queen Elizabeth to do all the damage possible to her enemies, the Spanish, he stopped at Cumana, St. Mary's, and Rio de la Hacha, and compelled them to furnish supplies for his fleet.

He had scarcely rested at home before he set about a second expedition to Guiana. This he intrusted to Captain Keymis, one of the captains of the first expedition. On his arrival he found the mouth of the River Caroni in possession of a party of Spaniards, under the direction of De Berreo, and his way to the mines effectually blocked. But he went on exploring the country, beyond the range of Raleigh's observations; and returned in a few months, with valuable additions to their geographical knowledge.

Persisting in his purpose of adding Guiana to the English possessions, he makes a further appeal to the public, in a pamphlet entitled "Of a Voyage to Guiana," on the ground that "by this means infinite numbers of souls may be brought from their idolatry, bloody sacrifices, ignorance, . and incivility, to the worshiping aright of the true God, and to civil conversation. This will stop the mouths of the Roman Catholics, who boast of their great adventures for the propagation

7

of the Gospel; it will add great increase of honor
to the memory of Her Majesty's name upon earth
to all posterity; and in the end be rewarded with
an excellent starlight splendency in the heavens,
which is reserved for them that turn many unto
righteousness, as the prophet speaketh." Not
finding any support from government, he fits out
at his own expense another small ship, under the
command of Captain Leonard Perry, in 1596;
and in 1598 he had engaged the Duke of Finland
to join him with twelve ships to establish a colony
in Guiana; but by some means not now known
this scheme proved abortive. Nothing more was
attempted during the reign of Elizabeth.

The noble conduct of Raleigh in these enter-
prises completely restored him to the favor of the
queen; though the envy and ill-will of some people were thereby excited against him.

Chapter X.

NAVAL EXPEDITION AGAINST CADIZ—THE ISLAND'S ENTER-
PRISE—BREACH WITH ESSEX.

IN 1596 Lord Admiral Howard revived a
Scheme of attacking Cadiz, first suggested by
Sir John Hawkins in 1587, which was made so
effectual that in the sequel it was more advan-
tageous to England than the destruction of the
Armada. At first it was embarrassed by the hes-
itation of the queen as to whom she should in-
trust the command. At length her personal
favoritism of Essex decided in his favor. Lord
Admiral Howard was made second in command,
and Sir Walter Raleigh and Lord Thomas Howard were ranked next in order. The fleet numbered one hundred and twenty-one ships, including twenty-four Dutch ships, besides pinnaces and
barges, and was divided into four separate squadrons. The whole number of sailors and soldiers

was sixteen thousand.   The principal object was
the destruction of the Spanish navy and the
seizure of rich merchant ships, rather than the
taking of Cadiz.   This agreed with the judgment
of Sir Walter Raleigh.   Some delay was made by
the repugnance of the soldiers and sailors who
were pressed into the service. Desertions took
place every day, until some of them were tried
by martial law and hung, which had the effect to
intimidate the rest and secure subordination.

Early in June the fleet left Plymouth Sound,
and arrived off Cadiz on the 20th of this month.
The harbor was defended by about eighty war-
vessels, including twenty galleys. Essex prepared
to land the soldiers, and immediately attack the
fort; but a council of war was objecting, when
Raleigh, having arrived from some excursion,
joined in the objections, and it was finally concluded to attack the ships of war.   Raleigh was
ordered to lead the assault.   As soon as day
began to break he started in the *War Spright*,
followed by the ships of his squadron. Passing
the galleys, which he regarded but as "masks,"

he made directly for the *Philip* and the *Andrew*, the leading ships, and the two largest in the Spanish navy. For three hours he battled with both of them, and then determined to board the *Philip*, and end the fight in that way. But the order was not to board without the aid of the flyboats, and they were not come. At that moment he saw the flag-ship of Essex approaching, and flinging himself into a skiff, he rowed to him, and demanded permission to board at once. Essex tried to persuade him against taking so great a hazard, but finally bade him do as he would, saying, "I will second you, upon my honor." He returned to his ship, and brought her into position to board, when the *Philip* drew back, and ran aground. Her crew sprang into the sea, and she was blown up. Sir Walter then turned to engage other ships, and succeeded in taking two, the *St. Andrew* and *St. Matthew*, which were afterward brought to England—the only ships captured that were not destroyed. The whole naval battle, of which we have only a glimpse, went on in the same fashion. Sir Walter compared it to "hell itself." The victory of the English was complete. Thirteen war ships and seventeen galleys were taken or destroyed.

Cadiz is built upon a peninsula, and it was now the first object of the English to prevent all communication with the mainland. The soldiers were landed, and, headed by Essex, made an assault upon the nearest gate. Raleigh had been wounded in the naval battle; but he was borne on a litter into the fight, and was one of the first that entered into the captured town. With the town the whole of the merchant ships in the harbor and their stores fell. An offer of two millions of ducats was accepted from the merchants of Cadiz and Seville as ransom for the India fleet that then lay at Puerte Real; but the fleet was set on fire by the Duke of Medina. One hundred and twenty thousand ducats was offered for the ransom of the lives of the combatants in the city, and fifty persons were delivered as hostages for its payment; but the money not being paid, the hostages were carried prisoners to England. The fortifications of Cadiz and much of the town was rased to the ground.   But nobody was killed or abused after the surrender, but all the captives were carried to the Port of St. Mary.

The people of England were in raptures over this great victory, and many a home was made glad by the return of friends who had been prisoners of war and slaves in the Spanish galleys. Great quarreling ensued in respect to the spoils by the parties concerned, and rumor told falsehood if Queen Elizabeth was not the most grasping of all.   The wife of Admiral Howard writes, "It was told me certainly that my lord should have his part, five thousand pounds, and Sir Walter Raleigh three thousand pounds; but being at court yesterday, I heard that the queen claimed all, and my Lord of Essex, it is thought, will yield his right to her majesty.   My lord hath spent already twenty thousand pounds in the queen's service."

It was the year after these events that Raleigh was reinstated in his old office of captain of the guard.   At first Essex received him coldly, but after a while their friendly relations were re sumed. Cecil, who was now Secretary of State, had contributed to the restoration of Raleigh, and an endeavor was made on his part to reconcile Essex to Cecil, but not with the greatest success.

This year was marked by another expedition against the Spaniards. It was rumored that Philip II had determined on creating another Armada more invincible than the former, wherewith to assail the English. Sir Walter Raleigh wrote a pamphlet upon the subject, in which he expresses the opinion that it was not to be believed that the King of Spain should attempt such a thing after the disasters he had already experienced; nevertheless he advised that the nation should be prepared for any event by suitable defenses along the coast. Moreover, he proposes that the initiative should be taken by an expedition against the Spanish navy and commerce. This new enterprise was called the Island's Voyage, as it resulted in the conquest of the Azores. It was at first intended to equip ten ships, and place them under the joint command of Raleigh and Lord Thomas Howard; but the plan was afterward much enlarged, and three squadrons were fitted out, commanded by Essex as admiral, with Lord Thomas Howard as vice-admiral, and Raleigh as rear-admiral. With these joined a Dutch squadron of twelve ships, commanded by Admiral Van der Woord. This great fleet put out to sea from Plymouth Sound on the 10th of July, 1597, but was soon overtaken by a terrific tempest, which came near sinking them altogether, and so disabled several of the best ships that they were all obliged to put back to various ports for repairs. It was afterward concluded to leave the land forces, and rely exclusively upon the ships.

The 17th of August found them again afloat, and proceeding to the coast of Spain. Off Cape Ortegal they encountered another terrible gale blowing directly out of the port of Ferrol. A council of war was called, and it was agreed to abandon the project of attacking Ferrol and Corunna, and proceed to the Azores. Sir Walter's ship was disabled, and he could not keep up with the movements of the fleet; but at length he joined it at Flores, one of the Azores, in latitude 36° to 39°. Essex was enraged at the absence of Raleigh, and had written to England, charging him with treachery and desertion. This he frankly and regretfully confessed when he found his mistake. Subsequently a collision took place in respect to the assault upon Fayal. The order was for Raleigh to support Essex; but it happened that Raleigh arrived three days before Essex, and waiting all that time, and not knowing what had happened to the admiral, he landed his men, and captured the place. When challenged for breach of order, he defended himself by quoting an article in the orders, which run: "No captain of any ship or company, if he be severed from the fleet, shall wend anywhere without directions from the general or *some other principal commander*, upon pain of death." Lord Thomas Howard interposed between the commanders, and the apology was accepted; but much ill feeling continued to exist between them, fomented by Sir Christopher Blount and other influential adherents of Essex, who were unfriendly to Raleigh.

To persons so disposed, envy had much provocation in the matter of this attack on Fayal, for it was one of the most brilliant exploits of Sir Walter. While waiting for Essex in the harbor of Hoctu, the chief town of the island, Sir Walter sought to improve the time to take in water. While about this business, he was fired upon by the garrison, which so excited his sailors that they demanded to be led to the assault. Taking his ship as near the shore as was convenient, he took two hundred and fifty men, and attempted to land them in barges on the rock-bound shore. The Spanish forces lined the shore, and opened such a fire upon them that a panic seized his men, and they began to push back, when Raleigh, shouting to them to follow him, shoved his barge forward toward a narrow passage between the rocks, where a landing was practicable. The retreating sailors rallied, and the whole force rushed to his support; and being joined by other barges from the Netherland squadron, the Spanish troops retreated into the woods, and left the town an easy prey to the victors. Sir Gilly Merrick had objected to the storming of the town, and he represented that it was done to deprive the admiral of the honor of the exploit. Besides the taking of these islands, the fleet captured eighteen Spanish vessels, including several very rich prizes. Raleigh's squadron fell in with a very rich carack, and would have taken it as a prize; but the crew set it on fire, and escaped in boats, while Raleigh in vain attempted to extinguish the flames. A Spanish squadron, sent forth from Ferrol, was overtaken by a storm and sunk. So Providence interfered for the protection of England.

"'The Islands' Voyage" would have been a failure but for the part which Raleigh took in it. His reputation was enhanced by it, and he became chief among the counselors of the queen in her relations to Spanish affairs. He constantly advises that the power of Spain must be guarded against, not by costly bulwarks on the English coast, but by ships of war and naval expeditions against her commerce, her extended colonies, and her maritime ports. In after years he wrote, "If the late queen would have believed her men of war as she did her scribes, we had, in her time, beaten that great empire to pieces, and made their kings kings of figs and oranges as in old times. But her majesty did all by halves, and by petty invasions taught the Spaniard how to defend himself, and to see his own weakness, which, till our attempts taught him, was hardly known to him-self. Four thousand men would have taken from him all the ports of his Indies; I mean all his ports by which his treasure doth or can pass. He is more hated in that part of the world by the sons of the conquered than are the English by the Irish."

Chapter XI.

RALEIGH AND HIS COMPEERS AT COURT—REVOLT AND EXECUTION OF ESSEX.

RALEIGH and Essex were now much together in the court and councils of Queen Elizabeth, and though they never were affected with cordial friendship for each other, yet they harmonized in conduct, and on one marked occasion, Raleigh was of much service to the Earl. While Essex was prosecuting the Cadiz expedition, Robert Cecil was made Secretary of State, at which Essex took offense, especially because he had recommended for that office Sir Thomas Bodley, the founder of the Bodleian Library at Oxford University. He also was annoyed and humiliated by the bestowment of the Earldom of Nottingham upon Lord Howard, as a reward for his services in the recent naval expeditions; inasmuch as this elevation, in connection with his office of lord high admiral, gave him, according to the statutes,

the precedence over Essex.   Raleigh found no
way to adjust this delicate matter but to suggest
to the queen to create Essex earl marshal of
England.   This she did; but it gave offense to
Nottingham, and he withdrew for a time from
court to his estate in Chelsea.

All this time it seems that Essex was losing
somewhat the favor of the queen.   This down-
ward tendency was increased by the encouragement which Essex gave, contrary to the views of
the queen, to the marriage of the Earl of Southampton, one of her courtiers, to Elizabeth Vernon,
which resulted in his dismissal from court and
confinement for a time in the "Fleet" prison.
He afterward gave mortal offense to the queen,
in one of his angry moods, by contemptuous
words and gestures.   This she never forgave.

She was annoyed by the rivalry of Raleigh
and Essex.   This was displayed in an extraor-
dinary and even ridiculous manner, at a tourna-
ment given in honor of the queen's birthday.
On this occasion Raleigh was arrayed in a suit
of armor very splendid and costly, and the jewels

he wore were valued at a quarter of a million of dollars. He had a numerous retinue prepared for the second day's tilt arrayed in gorgeous apparel, with orange-colored feathers in their caps. Essex, being apprised of this, appeared in a suit of orange-color, followed by two thousand retainers adorned with orange-colored feathers!

The affairs of Ireland at this time were exciting great solicitude, and a leader was called for who should be able to subdue the rebellion that was rising in that unhappy country. Raleigh was the man to whom attention was first turned, but he declined altogether; and the choice wavered between Earl Essex and Charles Blount, now Lord Mountjoy. By the urgent solicitation of the latter, it was finally settled that Essex should be made Lord Deputy. He exulted in his success. "I have beaten Raleigh and Knollys in the council," he exclaimed, as he set out for Ireland, "and I will beat Sir Owen in the field; for nothing worthy of Her Majesty's honor has yet been achieved." Alas! this Irish expedition was the beginning of his ruin.

O'Neil, Earl of Tyrone, instigated by the pope and the King of Spain, had commenced the rebellion with a formidable body of troops, and to meet and subdue him was the first object to be gained. Essex, however, turned aside to suppress an outbreak in Munster, and was so far disabled by the conflict that he thought it prudent not to attack Tyrone, but to negotiate with him. This transaction was denounced at court, and a very sharp altercation by letters took place, which induced him to quit his command to defend himself in person.

When he arrived at the court, without changing his apparel, he rushed into the queen's bedchamber, and fell down on his knees to plead with her. But his case was submitted to a council, and resulted in his being deprived of his office, and all other public positions except that of master of the horse.

Soon after this he engaged in correspondence with the King of Scotland, in respect of procuring a public recognition of his right to the English crown on the demise of Elizabeth. He corresponded also with Lord Mountjoy, now Deputy of Ireland, to induce him to employ the troops under his command to enforce this measure. He conspired, furthermore, to seize the queen's person, and revolutionize the government.

Finding that his schemes were discovered and exposed, he made an effort to incite the populace of London in his favor, and his intention was by their aid to make his way to the presence of the queen. Raleigh sent a messenger to one of his old friends, Sir Ferdinand Gorges, to meet him at Durham House. Essex was consulted about this, and he advised Gorges to go by water, but not to land at the Durham House. At this interview Sir Walter advised him of his danger, and exhorted him to go at once to his post as governor of Plymouth. Sir Ferdinand thanked him for his advice, but stated that he was engaged another way. Upon being asked what he meant he said "there were two thousand gentlemen who had resolved this day to die, or live freemen." Raleigh expressed surprise, and they parted.

To Essex the queen sent a deputation of four privy councilors, the lord keeper, and the chief justice, to inquire about what was intended by these movements. They found him surrounded by a turbulent crowd, and attended by several nobles of distinction, and other gentlemen. He ordered the commissioners into custody, and went forth into the streets, to promote in person the rising of the populace. To his dismay, there was no indication of popular sympathy, when word came of the approach of a strong force under the command of the lord admiral. Turning to regain his house, he found his way barricaded, and was obliged to take boats and come by the river. He set about fortifying his house; but it was soon surrounded by the queen's troops, and at midnight he was induced to surrender, and was taken to Lambeth Palace, and the next day to the Tower.

He was soon after arraigned at Westminster Hall, and charged with treason. The sergeant-at-law, Yelverton, in his argument, compared him to Catiline, and Coke, the attorney of the crown, insinuated that he aimed to become king of England. Essex protested that he meant no more than to force his way to the presence of the queen, to counteract the machinations of his enemies. He was condemned to be beheaded, and in seven days after the trial this sentence was executed. Raleigh was present as captain of the guard, and for that he was charged by his enemies as exulting in the death of his rival. He subsequently protested that, so far from rejoicing, he "shed tears at his death," and he was observed to be deeply sad as he returned in a boat from the Tower. Was it a forecast of his own destiny?

It was expected that the queen would pardon Essex; but, though she was terribly affected by his sad fate, she made no sign of interference. She had given him a ring, in the days of his prosperity, with the promise that she would pardon any offense, if he presented it to her. This ring was in the possession of the Countess of Nottingham, but her husband forbade her returning it. This, on her death-bed, she confessed to the queen. Elizabeth turned pale, and trembled

Queen Elizabeth giving a Ring to Essex.

with grief and indignation at this confession, and said "God might forgive her, but she never could!"

Sir Christopher Blount was tried for his participation in this conspiracy, and was condemned to be beheaded on the scaffold. He inquired, "Is Sir Walter Raleigh here?" When Sir Walter came near he said: "Sir Walter Raleigh, I thank God that you are present. I had an infinite desire to speak with you, to ask your forgiveness, ere I died. But for the harm done you, and for my particular ill intent toward you, I beseech you to forgive me." Raleigh replied, "I most willingly forgive you, and I beseech God to forgive you, and to give you his divine comfort." Sir Christopher had exhorted Gorges to seize the person of Raleigh on the occasion of their interview on the Thames; and he had himself, in the streets of London, shot at Raleigh four times, with intent to kill him.

Essex was but thirty-four years of age at his death. He was born, according to the astrologers, under the "disastrous aspect of Mars shining adversely upon him, in the eleventh house of heaven." It is said that his footman, on his death-bed, warned him that that year would be a fatal one to him. With all his faults he had a generous heart, and was a friend to the common people, who mourned his death.

Chapter XII.

RALEIGH GOVERNOR OF JERSEY — HIS DOMESTIC LIFE —
MEMBER OF PARLIAMENT—HIS LITERARY ASSOCIATES.

I T was in 1600 that Raleigh was made governor
of Jersey. This island is interesting to American readers as having given its name to one of
the original thirteen United States. It is situated
in the English Channel, the largest and most
southern of that group of islands, lying about
seventeen miles from the coast of France, which
belongs to Great Britain. It is twelve miles long,
by an average of six and a half miles broad. Its
climate is delightfully mild and salubrious, and
its soil is fertile, especially adapted to producing
fruits of all kinds common to the Temperate
Zone. Many remains of Druidical antiquities are
found there: the old churches are mostly of the
Gothic style; and the population is in religion
Roman Catholic. It is distant from England

seventy-five miles.   Lady Raleigh writes concerning her husband's first visit to the island: "He
was two days and two nights on the sea, with
contrary winds, notwithstanding he went from
Weymouth with so fair wind and weather as little
Wat and myself brought him on board the ship.
He writeth to me that he never saw a pleasanter
island; but protested unfeignedly that it was not
in value a third part of what was reported."

With characteristic zeal he set himself to work
for the benefit of the island.   He commenced a
system for the registration of the real estate,
opened a profitable trade with Newfoundland,
abolished the *corps de garde*, an oppressive military service imposed on the people, and, as judge
in civil courts, he exerted his influence to abate
the litigation to which the people of these peace-
ful islands seem to have been addicted.

Sir Walter's home in England was now at
Sherborne, in Devonshire.   Having failed to purchase the homestead where he was born, he obtained from Queen Elizabeth an estate which a
Norman knight bequeathed to the See of Canter-

bury, with a curse upon any profane person who should covet it. It was finally passed over to the Bishop of Salisbury, who ceded it to Elizabeth. When Raleigh went to see the place, it is related as a bad omen that his horse fell, and brought him on his face to the ground. But little did he care for such prognostic. He sprang up laughing, addressed his half-brother Gilbert, and with a joke turned it into a good omen. He ventured to make the place an elegant and happy home for his family. He built upon it a house surpassing, for beauty and convenience, all the mansions in that region. Here he enjoyed, when absent from Parliament and other public engagements, the society of his family, and the visits of his numerous literary and political friends. He was fondly attached to his wife and children, kind and generous to his servants, and abundant in hospitality. To fix his estate as a family inheritance, in 1602 he settled it upon his eldest son, Walter. His second son, Carew, was not yet born. We shall see how the conveyance of his estate was eventually made void by a clerical

error in the omission of a few words. The
principal inconvenience of this residence was
its distance from London, where his duties at
court and as a member of Parliament required
his presence much of the time. There were no
railroads in those days, and the post-roads were
not so perfect as they are now.

Sir Walter was member of Parliament for
Devonshire in 1585, and he was returned for
Cornwall in 1601, in the latter part of the reign
of Elizabeth. His brother-in-law, Sir Carew Gilbert, was also a member. He exhibited his characteristic energy and industry in the business of
committees, and in the debates on the floor of
the House of Commons. He distinguished himself by his successful objection to the act to promote the culture of hemp. On this occasion he
said: "I do not like this constraining of men to
manure the ground as one wills; but rather let
every man use his ground for that which it is
most fit for, and therein use his own discretion.
For when the law provides that every man must
plow the third of his land, I know divers poor

people have done so to avoid the penalty of the statute when their abilities have been so poor that they have not been able to buy seed corn to sow it; nay, they have been fain to hire others to plow it, which, if it had been unplowed, would have been good pasture for beasts, or might have been converted to still other uses." In 1593, he took part in the debate on subsidies. " On that occasion," says Edwards, "he entered into an elaborate review of the power and resources of Spain; showed that those resources extended virtually over Northern as well as Southern Europe; that in France Philip had effectual command of important towns and havens; and that even in Scotland he had 'so corrupted the nobility' that some of them had agreed to work with Spanish forces for the re-establishment of Papistry. 'In his own country,' continued Sir Walter, 'there is all possible preparation, and he is coming with sixty galleons, beside other shipping, with purpose to annoy us. If he invade us, we must have no ships riding at anchor. All will be little enough to withstand him. At his coming he fully resolv-

eth to get Plymouth, . . . and Plymouth is
in most danger.' And then he goes on to con-
tend, as he always contended, that the way to defeat Philip was not to wait for him. 'Let us send
a royal army to supplant him in Brittany, and to
possess ourselves there, and send also a strong
navy to sea, and to lie with it upon the cape and
such places as his ships bring his riches to, that
they may set upon all that come. This we are
able to do, and we shall undoubtedly have for-
tunate success if we undertake it.'"

It was such forcast as this speech indicates
which had before prepared the nation to meet
the invincible Armada when it came, and, by
the co-operation of nature in her hurricane and
storm, to sweep it to destruction.

On the subject of monopolies, by which it was
costomary to reward public services, Sir Walter
made a profound sensation by declaring his will-
ingness to resign his patent on the tin mines if
there should be a general repeal of licenses. One
who was present when his speech was delivered,
remarked that "there was a great silence after

it." The idea was adopted by Elizabeth, and she made her reign popular by the abolition of the most oppressive of these monopolies. Herein free trade, the glory and prosperity of England, began to dawn on the councils of the **State**.

Raleigh had doubts as to the matter of his own monopoly in the tin mines being any disadvantage on the whole, particularly because under his management the workmen were well paid, and regarded him with much affection. "Now I tell you," he said in the debate, "that before the granting of my patent, whether tin were but seventeen shillings and so up to fifty shillings a hundred, yet the poor workman never had but two shillings a week, finding himself. But since my patent, whosoever will work, be tin at what price sold, they have four shillings a week, truly paid. Notwithstanding, if all others be repealed, I will give my consent as freely to the canceling of this as any member of this House." The question of free trade in this country has been in debate from the beginning, and until lately it made a chief distinction between the leading political parties. The necessity of a vast revenue to pay the war debt has made large duties on imports inevitable, and the economical question is practically laid on the shelf.

As lieutenant of Cornwall, Raleigh devoted himself to the welfare of the county, and especially of the common people. He resisted successfully an attempt of some politicians to get an old tax on the curing of fish restored; he also succeeded in getting the tax upon tin considerably reduced. "Your ears and mouth have ever been open to hear and deliver our grievances," wrote Richard Carew in his Survey of Cornwall, "and your feet and hands ready to go and work their redress; and that not only as a magistrate of yourself, but also very often as a suitor and solicitor to others of the highest place." Unpopular as he was with the politicians, and oftentimes exciting the ill will of the London populace, and especially the party of Essex, Raleigh was admired and loved by his own neighbors, and by the soldiers and sailors who served under him.

While residing on his estates, he devoted much

leisure time to antiquarian researches, and to mineralogical observations and studies. His mind was ever active, and his tongue and pen and hands were unceasingly active.

He was a member of the antiquarian society formed under Archbishop Parker in 1572. He instituted a club of literary men in London, who held their meetings at a tavern called the Mermaid, in Friday Street. It was composed of such men as Shakespeare, Beaumont, Fletcher, Ben Jonson, Selden, Cotton, Carew, Martin, Donne, and others, whose names are yet stars in the horizon of letters. ".Many," says Fuller, "were the wit combats between Ben Jonson and Shakespeare. I beheld them like a Spanish great galleon and an English man-of-war. Master Jonson, like the former, was built far higher in learning, solid, but slow in his performances. Shakespeare, like the latter, lesser in bulk, but lighter in sailing, could turn with all tides, tack about, and take advantage of all winds by the quickness of his wit and invention."

Chapter XIII.

DEATH OF ELIZABETH—ACCESSION OF JAMES—HIS CHAR-
ACTER AND WORKS—RALEIGH'S DISGRACE AT COURT—
CHARGED WITH CONSPIRACY—IMPRISONMENT IN THE
TOWER.

QUEEN Elizabeth died on 24th day of March, 1602, in the seventieth year of her age, and the forty-fifth of her reign. The death of Essex made a melancholy impression upon her mind, which she could not throw off, and which, to-gether with State cares—the discussions about the succession—affected her health and hastened her end. Having a good constitution and the most temperate habits, she disdained the use of medicine. Feeling that her days were numbered, she devoted herself to religious meditations and exercises. That she might enjoy these without so much molestation, she left Westminster, and re-paired to Richmond. She had the attendance and ministrations of the Archbishop of Canterbury, and to him she communicated her inmost feelings in regard to her relations to the eternal life, and to her successor on the throne. Vexed by the intrigues which she saw going on around her, she kept silence in regard to her decision in respect to the succession until the last hours of her life, when she declared to Lord Howard, of Effingham, her faithful friend, "that her throne had been the throne of kings, and that her kinsman, the King of Scots, should succeed her." After this she abandoned herself to prayer, that her mind might be, as she expressed it, "wholly fixed on God." Thus died the maiden queen, than whom no greater ruler ever occupied the throne of England.

While before the death of Elizabeth the question of succession was under discussion, Raleigh and Cecil took opposite views. Raleigh was opposed to the King of Scotland, and preferred the claims of Arabella Stuart, who was the fourth in descent from Henry VII. Her father, the Earl of Lenox, was the grandson of Margaret Tudor, who was the daughter of Henry VII. She was

9

born in England, and was, like James, a Protestant. Elizabeth at first seemed to be friendly to Arabella, and instructed her embassador to propose her marriage with James, and end the question; but afterward, for some reason unexplained, she turned against Arabella, and her opposition was intensified by that lady's projected marriage to William Seymour, afterward Duke of Somerset, who also was a descendant of Henry VII. When James was acknowledged to be the rightful heir to the crown, and came to London to establish his court, he regarded the friends of Arabella with jealousy, and was particularly evil-disposed toward Sir Walter Raleigh. He suspected him to be the author of certain pamphlets in opposition to his claims, and to have been concerned in the condemnation and execution of his friend, the unfortunate Earl of Essex. Cecil seems to have encouraged this disposition in James, and to stand altogether in his light as he approached the new monarch for the usual congratulations and welcomes expected of courtiers. On their first interview, James, in the broadest Northern dialect,

returned his salutation with a poor grace, "On
my soul, mon, I have heard *Rawly* of thee."
He accepted the presents of Raleigh; but his
timidity and love of peace was unpleasantly affected by Raleigh's bold and generous, but ill-
advised, offer to support, at his own expense, a
force of two thousand men to invade the territo-
ries of Spain.   This offer was the key-note, as we
shall see, of a disastrous tenor of events, that
brought the brave knight to an untimely and
cruel end.

James I of England and VI of Scotland was
the son of the beautiful but unfortunate Mary,
Queen of Scotland.   His father was Henry Stuart,
Lord Darnley, the cousin and husband of Mary,
with whom she was, at the time of James's birth,
at variance, having fixed her affection on the Earl
of Bothwell.   The assassination of Darnley followed, and Bothwell was suspected of being the
instigator of the deed; nevertheless the impru-
dent queen married him.   The result was a rebellion against the authority of the queen, which
drove Bothwell into exile in Denmark, and Mary

to imprisonment in the Castle of Loch Leven. She escaped; a battle ensued at Langside; her army was defeated; she fled to England; was kept a prisoner eighteen years by Elizabeth, at the end of which she was charged with conspiracy against the crown; was tried, condemned, and beheaded, February 8, 1587.

James was crowned King of Scotland while yet an infant, and was kept in Stirling Castle, under the regency of the Earl of Mar. His tutor was the celebrated Buchanan, and he proved a diligent scholar in the learning of the times. He early imbibed inflated notions of royal supremacy; and by his arrogance he set his nobles against him, and a party took possession of his person, and confined him in Ruthven Castle. A counter revolution soon effected his liberation, and he was placed under the tutorship of his favorite, the unprincipled Earl of Arran. He showed little sympathy for his unhappy mother until her life was in danger, when he protested against the course Elizabeth was pursuing, and appealed to other courts of Europe for interference. At her death his nobles were ready to make war on the English nation, but the poverty of his resources prevented it.   When Philip II threatened the invasion of England, his decided and ardent Protestantism prompted him to forego personal animosity and to offer his assistance to repel the invasion.

He was thirty-seven years of age when the death of Elizabeth in 1603 opened his way, by hereditary claim, to the crown of England.   His progress to London was cheered by the popular acclamations, and he distributed the honors and titles at his disposal with the greatest profusion on Englishmen and Scotchmen.

It is said that his timidity was such that, when he laid his sword on the shoulder of the new-made knight, he averted his eyes.   He had also a habit of rolling his eyes after any person who was introduced to him, which was very embarrassing to strangers.

He held a conference at Hampton Court between the Puritans and the divines of the English Church, in which he displayed a bitter hostility to innovations on the established order of the

Church, and to all kinds of non-conformity. He did not pursue the non-conformist with the sword and fagot, as in the previous reign; but he expelled the Puritans from their offices in the Church, and in 1604 no less than three hundred pastors were silenced, imprisoned, or banished. As to the Catholics, he disappointed their expectations of royal favor; and their despair of gaining any thing from him or his Parliament led, in 1605, to the Gunpowder Plot, the object of which was to annihilate at a blow the king and the Parliament.

Catesby, Percy, and some other papists, devised the plan of storing gunpowder under the Parliament Hall, to be fired when the session should be opened, at which time the king and royal family would be present. More than twenty persons had the fatal secret; but it was kept until within ten days of the appointed time, when a Catholic peer received a note advising him not to attend Parliament if he would avoid a calamity. This he carried to Lord Salisbury, Secretary of State, and the matter was at once made known to King James. Salisbury made light of it; but the timidity and sagacity of the king prompted him to order a thorough search of the vaults of the Hall, where both houses of Parliament assembled. At the door Guy Fawkes was found with matches in his pocket, and two hogsheads and thirty-six barrels of gunpowder were discovered. Guy Fawkes, on being put to torture, confessed the plot and all the persons concerned in it. These conspirators, with their attendants, to the number of eighty, concentrated at Warwickshire, and determined to defend themselves against arrest. Catesby and Percy were killed in the attack, and the residue were captured, tried, and executed.

In the Calendar of the Church of England the 5th of November is made a holiday; and the boys in England, and even in Boston, Massachusetts, celebrated it by carrying about an effigy of Guy Fawkes, singing, as they burnt it:

"Remember, remember
The fifth of November,
Gunpowder treason and plot!

We know no reason
Why gunpowder treason
Should ever be forgot.
Hallo, boys! Hurra!"

The truly great and the only great deed which distinguishes the reign of James was the translation of the original Scriptures into the English. At the Hampton conference, which displayed the intolerance of the king, the leader of the nonconformists was Dr. Reynolds, who has the honor of having suggested to the king the necessity of this translation. The king at once perceived its importance, and orders were issued the next year, 1604, appointing fifty-four distinguished scholars to do the work. Seven of them, however, for some reason, failed to be actually employed in it. These were divided into six classes, to each of which was assigned a distinct portion of the Scriptures, to be translated by each member of the class, and to be revised by the whole class, and then sent to the other classes for examination. These translations employed three years. The whole work was then sent to London, and

was revised by a committee of one from each
of the six classes, and finally criticised by Dr.
Smith and Bishop Bilson. It was finally printed
in 1611. This is admitted to be the noblest of
all translations of the Bible, scarcely inferior in
spirit and letter to the inspired original. Re-
cently a convention of learned men have been
employed on a revision of King James's version,
which is designed to correct what errors of translation have been observed in it, without alteration
of its general style.

The ill will of James to Raleigh was soon
revealed by an act of oppression in reference to
his eldest son, Walter Raleigh, Jr. This young
man was engaged to a wealthy heiress, Miss
Basset, a descendant of the Plantagenets. This
engagement was broke up by James, and the
young lady compelled to marry Henry Howard.
Her relative, Sir Robert Basset, opposed this
transaction so vehemently that he was made an
object of the royal displeasure, and his estate
was confiscated, and he was compelled to flee
the country to save his life.

The Earl of Southampton, who was an accomplice of Essex in his conspiracy against Elizabeth, was called from the Tower, and received with favor by the king, while Sir Walter was informed that his presence was not acceptable. This maneuver was attributed by Raleigh to the malicious influence of Cecil, and he wrote a letter to the king, in which he blamed Cecil for the execution of Essex, and charged him with having brought about the execution of Queen Mary, against the intention and wishes of Elizabeth. This made Cecil his implacable enemy. Sir Walter also joined with others to advise a limitation of the prerogatives of the king, and moderation in bestowing honors upon those favorites who were not natives of England. This was an unpardonable offense to one who was inflated with notions of kingly right and privilege—notions, which bequeathed to his son and successor, Charles I, brought him to the block.

Before the accession of James, the Catholics had much dispute among themselves as to the succession. Much hope was entertained of Spanish influence with the prospective king, procuring for their Church great toleration and larger privileges, and agents were sent to the court of Scotland for furthering these views. William Watson and Francis Clarke, Catholic priests, were the most prominent of these emissaries. James acted a double part in dealing with this question. To the pope he intimated that his accession to the throne of England would be an advantage to the Papists, while to the English court he expressed his dissatisfaction with the leniency and favor shown to them. Three weeks before his arrival in England a scheme for seizing his person was communicated by Sir Griffin Markham, a Catholic gentleman, to his two trustees, whom he had invited to dine with him at Berwood Park. He led them into the depths of the woods, and bound them by an oath not to reveal what he was about to relate. He then told them that a band of men had entered into a conspiracy to surprise the king at Greenwich, and to bring him to the Tower, which a party of them was to seize for that purpose. Among them were George Brooke,

brother to Lord Cobham, Anthony Capley, a Cath
olic gentleman, and Lord Grey, of Wilton.   Lord
Grey was a Puritan, and hated Popery; but he
hated the Scotch more, and, like the Catholics,
longed for greater liberty in both civil and religious matters than could be hoped for from the
Scottish king.   The original design of surprising
the king at Greenwich was laid aside for a plan
of seizing him on his departure from Hanworth.
It was much against Priest Watson's judgment
that such a Protestant nobleman as Lord Grey
should be mixed up with the scheme, and so he
invented a plot within the plot to capture the
king from Lord Grey and his troop, and to carry
him to the Tower as if for safe keeping from his
enemies, and by this means to secure the favor
of the king to the Catholic cause.   He first revealed his plan to Sir Edward Parham, who fell
in with it at once.   But in various ways the
scheme of surprising the king was betrayed to
the king's council, and they took immediate
measures to guard the king's person. · Capley
was first arrested, and afterward the rest of the

conspirators.   It does not appear that Cobham had any thing to do with this "treason of the priests."   His brother had spoken of him to Watson, and of Sir Walter Raleigh, as discontented with the king, as well as Lord Grey.

The project of Cobham was a different affair altogether.   He had always been opposed to Essex and his views of the succession of the Scottish king.   He favored at first the right of the Lady Arabella; but after his introduction to her personally at the court of Elizabeth, for some reason, he changed his mind.   "When I saw her," he remarked to Cecil, "I resolved never to hazard my estate for her."

The correspondence of Cobham and Count d'Aremberg, Embassador of Archduke Albert, Sovereign of the Spanish Low Countries, is veiled in some obscurity; but it seems to have been respecting a treaty of peace with Spain, for which the influence of Cobham was solicited.   In their intimacies, Cobham told Raleigh about a sum of money which he hoped to receive for negotiations in this matter.   This being known by some means to the king's counselors, Cobham was suspected of some treasonable designs of his own, or complicity with the priests' conspiracy, and Sir Walter Raleigh was supposed to know something about it.

One day Cecil met Raleigh at Windsor, and notified him that the lords of the privy council had something to inquire of him. He was asked what he knew about a correspondence of Cobham with Aremberg, the Austrian embassador, in respect to Spanish affairs, the object of which was to induce Raleigh to favor an alliance of England with Spain. Raleigh denied that Cobham had any unwarrantable communication with himself or the Austrian minister, and referred the council to Laurencie, an Antwerp merchant, who had first introduced Cobham to Aremberg. Lord Cobham was afterward called before the council, and he entirely exonerated Raleigh from any improper transactions. After that, by an infamous artifice, a letter of Raleigh addressed to Cecil was shown to Cobham, from some expressions of which he was led to conclude that Raleigh had betrayed him. Whereupon, as if possessed with a demoniac

spirit of revenge he cried out, "O traitor! O vil-
lain! now will I confess the whole truth."   He
then confessed that his intention was to go to
Spain, and borrow six hundred thousand crowns
of Philip III, to pay the troops to be employed in
the conspiracy, and that he was to return by Jersey, where he would meet Raleigh, and arrange
for the disbursement of the money.   He further
deposed that it was by the instigation of Raleigh
that he embarked in this plot.   On being questioned, he declared ignorance of any other plots,
and contradicted his previous statements by stating
that he feared that, on arriving at Jersey, Raleigh would deliver him and his money into the
hands of the government.   He was then discharged; but before he reached the stairway to
depart, he was seized with remorse, and returned
and retracted all that he had said against his
friends.   His deposition had been taken in writing; but he refused to sign it.   He was constrained, however, to do so by being informed by
the chief justice that it would be treated as contempt of court.   Some weeks after he was newly

examined, and distinctly retracted his accusation of Sir Walter. Cecil, who never fully declared his conviction of Sir Walter Raleigh's complicity with the conspirators, but seems quite willing to find proof of it against his former friend, and in his letters makes the most of incidental matters, which might look unfavorable, now ascribes this change in Cobham to a correspondence which Raleigh contrived to have with Cobham in the confinement in neighboring apartments of the Tower. This was brought to the attention of Cobham; that he saw Sir John Paxton talking with Sir Walter at the window, and that, when he came to see him shortly after, he said to him, "I saw you with Sir Walter Raleigh. God forgive him! He hath accused me, but I can not accuse him." Then Sir John said, "He doth say the like of you: that you have accused him, but he can not accuse you." Cobham was mistaken about Raleigh's accusing him; it was his own brother Brooke that made the first disclosures of the plot.

Upon his first entrance into the Tower, Sir

"Walter Raleigh gave way to desponding thoughts. He knew he was innocent; but he had read history so as to convince him that the slightest things are taken for proofs of treason, and the innocent are condemned with the guilty. He knew the law was such that, if sentence was pronounced against him, it would result in the confiscation of his estate, and leave his wife and family destitute. Dwelling upon these considerations, he was so wrought up that he determined not to be brought to trial by sacrificing his life. On the 20th of July, 1603, while Lord Cecil was in the Tower examining the prisoners, he stabbed himself near the right breast. Cecil writes about it: "Although lodged and attended as well as in his own house, yet one afternoon, while divers of us were in the Tower examining these prisoners, Sir Walter Raleigh attempted to have murdered himself. Whereof, when we were advertised, we came to him, and found him in some agony, seeming to be unable to endure his misfortune, and protesting his innocency with carelessness of life. In that humor he had

10

wounded himself under the right pap, but no way mortally; being in truth rather a cut than a stab."

The following letter, lately found among State papers, and published in Edwards's second volume' reveals the feeling which moved him to this rash act:

TO LADY RALEIGH.

"Receive from thy unfortunate husband these, his last lines; these, the last words thou shalt ever receive from him. That I can live to see thee and my child more!—I can not. I have desired God and disputed with my reason, but nature and compassion hath the victory. That I can live to think how you are both left a spoil to my enemies, and that my name shall be a dishonor to my child,—I can not. I can not endure the memory thereof. Unfortunate woman, unfortunate child, comfort yourselves; trust God, and be contented in your poor estate. I would have bettered it, if I had enjoyed a few years.

"Thou art a young woman, and forbear not to marry again; thou art no more mine, nor I thine. To witness that thou didst love me once, take care that thou marry not to please sense, but to avoid poverty, and to preserve thy child. That thou didst also love me living, witness it to others; to my poor daughter, to whom I have given nothing; for his sake, who will be cruel to himself to preserve thee. Be charitable to her, and teach thy son to love her for his father's sake.

"For myself, I am left of all men that have done good to many. All my good turns forgotten; all my errors revived and expounded to all extremity of ill. All my services, hazards, and expenses for my country—plantings, discoveries, fights, councils, and whatsoever else—malice hath now covered over. I am now made an enemy and traitor by the word of an unworthy man. He hath proclaimed me to be a partaker of his vain imaginations, notwithstanding the whole course of my life hath approved the contrary, as my death shall approve it. Woe, woe, woe be unto him by whose falsehood we are lost! He hath separated us asunder. He hath slain my honor, my fortune. He hath robbed thee of thy husband, thy child of his father, and me of you both. O God, thou dost know my wrongs. Know then, thou my wife and child; know then, thou my lord and king,—that I ever thought them too honest to betray, and too good to conspire against.

"But, my wife, forgive them all, as I do. Live humble, for thou hast but a time also. God forgive my Lord Harry! for he was my heavy enemy. And for my Lord Cecil, I thought he would never forsake me in extremity. I would not have done it him, God knows. But do not thou know it; for he must be master of thy child, and may have compassion of him. Be not dismayed that I died in despair of God's mercies. Strive not to dispute it. But assure thyself that God hath not left me, nor Satan tempted me. Hope and Despair live not together. I know it is forbidden to destroy ourselves; but trust it is forbidden in this sort, that we destroy not ourselves despairing of God's mercy. The mercy of God is immeasurable; the cogitations of men comprehend it not.

"In the Lord I have ever trusted, and I know

that my Redeemer liveth.   Far is it from me to
be tempted with Satan.   I am only tempted with
sorrow, whose sharp teeth devour my heart.   O
God, thou art goodness itself.   Thou canst not
but be good to me.   O God, thou art mercy
itself.   Thou canst not but be merciful to me.

"For my estate, [it] is conveyed to feoffees—
to your cousin Brett and others.   I have but a
bare estate for a short life.   My plate is at gage
in Lombard Street; my debts are many   To
Peter Vanlove, some £600.   To Atropus as
much, but Compton is to pay £300 of it.   To
Michael Hext, £100.   To George Carew, £100.
To Nicholas Sanderson, £100.   To John Fitz-
james, £100.   To Master Waddon, £100.   To
a poor man, one Hawkes, for horses, £70.   To
a poor man called Hunt, £20.   Take first care
of those, for God's sake.   To a brewer at Weymouth, and a baker, for Lord Cecil's ship and
mine, I think some £80.   John Reynolds know-
eth it.   And let that poor man have his true part
of my return from Virginia; and let the poor
men's wages be paid with the goods, for the

Lord's sake. Oh, what will my poor servants think, at their return, when they hear I am accused to be Spanish, who sent them—at my great charge—to plant and discover upon his territory,

"Oh, intolerable infamy! O God, I can not resist these thoughts! I can not live to think how I am derided, to think of the expectation of my enemies, the scorns I shall receive, the cruel words of lawyers, the infamous taunts and despites, to be made a wonder and a spectacle! O Death, hasten thou unto me, that thou mayest destroy the memory of these, and lay me up in dark forgetfulness! O Death, destroy my memory, which is my tormentor! my thoughts and my life can not dwell in one body. But do thou forget me, poor wife, that thou mayest live to bring up my poor child.

"I recommend unto you my poor brother Gilbert. The lease of Tandridge is his, and none of mine. Let him have it, for God's cause. He knows what is due to me upon it. And be good to Kemis; for he is a perfect honest man, and hath much wrong for my sake. For the rest, I commend me to them, and them to God. And the Lord knows my sorrows to part from thee and my poor child. But part I must, by enemies and injuries; part with shame, and triumph of my detractors. And therefore be contented with this work of God, and forget me in all things but thine own honor and the love of mine.

"I bless my poor child; and let him know his father was no traitor. Be bold of my innocence; for God, to whom I offer life and soul, knows it. And whosoever thou choose again after me, let him but be thy politique husband. But let my son be thy beloved, for he is part of me, and I live in him; and the difference is but in the number, and not in the kind. And the Lord forever keep thee and them, and give thee comfort in both worlds!"

After Raleigh's recovery from his wound, he, like the other prisoners, was subjected to private examinations; but through all he confesses no guilt, and discloses nothing which betrays connection with the conspiracy. On the contrary,

Lord Grey confessed that he "had a part, a party, and confederates," and that their object was to take the king and his court by surprise. Brooke and Cobham made similar acknowledgments, and threw themsleves on the mercy of the king. Raleigh wrote an eloquent letter to the Earls of Nottingham, Suffolk, and Devonshire, and Lord Cecil, protesting his innocence, and showing reasons why he ought not to be confounded with the guilty. He wrote also supplicating letters to the king. He managed to hold a communication with Cobham, entreating him to exonerate him. He paid money to an attendant in the prison to throw an apple into Cobham's apartment, containing a letter to this effect. The answer was not altogether satisfactory. He then sent another letter in the same way, requesting Cobham at least to declare his innocence at the approaching trial. To this a reply came, plainly and solemnly declaring that Raleigh was innocent of all the charges.

As it happened that the plague was raging at London, and people were dying every-where—

except, strange to relate, in the Tower—it became necessary to remove the prisoners, for trial, to Winchester Castle.   Thither, in September, Raleigh was conveyed in his own coach, under the direction of Sir William Wade, who was, according to his own account, in constant alarm from the manifestation of popular ill-will toward his illustrious prisoners.   Mud and stones, and even tobacco-pipes, were thrown into the coach.   "He that had seen it," says Wade, "would not think there had been any sickness in London.   We took the best order we could in setting watches through all the streets, both in London and the suburbs.   If one hair-brain fellow among so great multitudes had begun to set on him, as they were very ready to do, no night-watch or means could have prevailed, the fury and tumult of the people were so great."   Raleigh seems never to have been popular with the masses, though very much beloved by his attendants, and by soldiers and sailors in his service.   The wrath of the populace, in this instance, was destined by the events of the trial to be converted into admiration and pity.

Chapter XIV.

THE TRIAL OF RALEIGH AND THE CONSPIRATORS—CONDUCT
OF SIR EDWARD COKE—THE SENTENCE OF THE PRISONERS.

THE plague, which made it necessary for the court to leave London, continued to rage until thirty thousand of the population perished. The king and his council repaired to Welton. A court of king's bench was prepared by the sheriff of Hants, at Wolverley Castle, the old episcopal Palace of Winchester. The trial of Sir Walter Raleigh commenced on the 17th of November, O. S. Cecil, Wade, and Henry Howard were made judges by special commission. With them were Lord Thomas Howard, Charles Blount, Edward Walton, Sir John Stanhope, Popham, lord chief-justice, Anderson, chief-justice of the common pleas, and two judges, Warburton and Gandy. Sir Edward Coke, attorney-general, was assisted by Sergeant Hale. The jury consisted of

knights, squires, and gentlemen, all strangers to
Raleigh. When the indictment was read, Sir
Walter pleaded, "Not guilty;" and when asked
if he had any objection to the jury, he answered,
"I know none of them, but think them all honest
and Christian men. I know my own innocence,
and, therefore, will challenge none. All are in-
different to me. Only this I desire: sickness
hath of late weakened me, and my memory is always bad; the points in the indictment are many,
and perhaps in the evidence more will be urged.
I beseech you, therefore, my lords, let me answer
the points severally as they are delivered, for I
shall not carry them all in my mind to the end."

Coke objected: "The king's evidence ought
not to be broken or dismembered, whereby it
might lose much of its grace and vigor." This
objection was overruled in part.

The indictment substantially was that he had
conspired against the government of the king;
had sought to excite sedition, to introduce the
Papal religion, and to engage foreign nations to
invade the kingdom. In addition to this con-

spiracy, he was charged with having published a book against the title of James, and had incited Lady Arabella Stuart to write to the King of Spain, to the Archduke of Austria, and to the Duke of Saxony to advance her title. Besides this he was implicated in transactions between Cobham and Aremburg, Embassador of Austria, to obtain five or six hundred thousand crowns from Philip III of Spain to aid the treason, of which Raleigh should have the disbursement of ten thousand crowns.

The opening of the case was made by Sergeant Hale, who displayed as much ability to manage such a case as could be expected from a small lawyer who could affirm, "As for the Lady Arabella, she, upon my conscience, hath no more title to the crown than I have, which before God I utterly renounce." As James himself could not trace a more direct relation to the royal line than Lady Arabella, Raleigh was seen to smile at the blundering witticism of the king's sergeant-at-law. Sir Edward Coke soon followed in turn, and made a display of mingled acuteness, eloquence,

effrontery, and malignity, which has left a blot
upon his character.   He declared that as no resort had been made to torture to extract the truth
from the conspirators, so he should bring nothing
but plain and positive proof against the prisoner.
He analyzed the crime charged in the following
pedantic manner: "Unto all great mischiefs,
there be ever three inseparable incidents.   The
first is *invitation;* the second, *supportation;* the
third, *defense.*   Within these three fall all Sir
Walter Raleigh's treasons.   For his is the treason
of '*the main;*' the others were '*the bye.*'   The
treason of '*the buy*' was that Lord Grey, Brooke,
Markham, and the others should hastily surprise
the king's court.   This was a rebellion in the
heart of the realm; yea, in the heart of the heart,
that is, the court.   They intended to break open
the doors with muskets, and so of a sovereign
make a subject.   Having him, they meant to
carry him to the Tower, and to keep him there
until they had extorted three things from him—
first, their own pardon; secondly, toleration for
the Romish superstition; and, thirdly, the re-

moval of certain privy councilors. This," he concluded, "was the treason of 'the buy.'"

Raleigh interposed, and addressed the jury: "I pray you, gentlemen of the jury, to remember that I am not charged with the 'buy,' which was the treason of the priests."

"You are not," replied Coke; "but your lordships will see that all these treasons, though they consisted of several points, closed in together, like Samson's foxes, which were joined in the tails, though the heads were severed."

He then went on reciting cases of treason in other reigns, and showing, too, or rather trying to show, that only one witness was necessary to make out a case of treason. He finally comes to the case. "Now, my masters of the jury, I come to your charge. Treason is of four kinds—treason *in corde* (in the heart), which is the root of the tree; treason *in ore* (in the mouth), which is the bud; treason *in manu* (in the hand), which is the blossom; and treason *in consummatione* (in consummation), which is the fruit. In this case you shall find the three first of these, these traitors being prevented before the consummation of their mischiefs.   But, though prevented, they are still traitors *in corde, in ore, et in manu.*"   And so he went on quoting Latin phrases, and charging the conspirators with the purpose not only to take the life of the king, but to destroy his posterity.   Then turning to Raleigh, he said, "But to whom, Sir Walter, did you bear malice?   To the royal children?"

"Master attorney," said Raleigh, "I pray you, to whom or to what end speak you all this?   I protest I do not understand what a word of this means, except it be to tell the news.   What is the treason of Markham and the priests to me?"

Coke replied, "I will, then, come close to you.   I will prove you to be the most notorious traitor that ever came to the bar.   They, indeed, are upon '*the main;*' but you followed them of 'the bye' in imitation.   I will charge you with the words."

"Your words can not condemn me," responded Raleigh.   "My innocence is my defense.   *Prove* against me any one thing of the many that you

have spoken, and I will confess all the indictment, and that I am the most horrible traitor that
ever lived, and worthy to be crucified with a
thousand torments."

"Nay," said Coke, "I will prove all. Thou
art a monster; thou hast an English face, but a
Spanish heart. You would have stirred England
and Scotland both. You incited the Lord Cobham, as soon as Count Aremberg came into England, to go to him. The night he went you
supped with Lord Cobham, and he brought you
after supper to Dunbar House; and then, the same
night, by a back way, went with La Renzi to
Count Aremberg, and got from him a promise
of the money. After this it was arranged that
Lord Cobham should go to Spain, and return by
Jersey." So he went on simply affirming the indictment.

Raleigh cried out, "Let me answer; it con-
cerns my life!"

Coke: "Thou shalt not."

Lord Chief Justice Popham then interposed,
saying: "Sir Walter Raleigh, master attorney is

yet but in general. But when the king's counsel hath given the whole evidence, you shall answer to every particular."

After this Coke went on stating that Cobham invented the scheme, but Raleigh was relied upon, both as a "politician and landsman," to manage and execute the plot; and that he contrived that Cobham should be the only witness against him, believing that he could not be convicted of treason by only one witness. He related several matters in which Cobham was concerned.

Raleigh replied: "What is this to me? I do not hear yet that you have spoken one word against me. If my Lord Cobham be a traitor, what is that to me?"

Coke retorted: "All that he did was by thy instigation, thou viper! for I *thou* thee, thou traitor! I will prove thee the rankest traitor in all England."

Raleigh replied that he might call him a traitor, but that was no proof of it. The lord chief-justice then charged them both to "be patient."

Coke then proceeded to give his proofs. It was simply a record of the examinations of Cobham, which was read by the clerk of the crown. Raleigh requested to look at it. Having done so, he addressed the jury in his defense. He explained that he was aware that Cobham, through La Renzi, had communications with Count Aremberg, and he informed Cecil of it, and that La Renzi should be called to account for it; but Cecil thought it not politic to do so, as the embassador might be offended; and that this letter was shown to Cobham, who in a sudden rage denounced him as a traitor, and then repented of it "ere he came to the stairs' foot, and acknowledged he had done wrong." He then turned to the attorney-general, and said, in language that thrilled every loyal and honest Englishman and Scotchman in the assembly:

"Master attorney, whether to favor or to disable my Lord Cobham, you speak as you will of him; yet he is not such a traitor as you make of him. He hath dispositions of such violence, which his best friends could never temper. But it is very strange that I, at this time, should be thought to plot with the Lord Cobham, knowing him a man that hath neither love or following; and myself, at this time, having resigned a place of my best command in an office I had in Cornwall, I was not so bare of sense but I saw that, if ever this state was strong, it was now that we have the kingdom of Scotland united, whence we were wont to fear all our troubles; Ireland quieted, where our forces were wont to be divided; Denmark assured, whom before we were always wont to have in jealousy; the Low Countries our nearest neighbor.   And, instead of a lady whom time had surprised, we had now an active king, who would be present at his own business.   For me at this time to make myself a Robin Hood, a Wat Tyler, a Kett, or a Jack Cade!   I was not so mad.   I knew the state of Spain well; his weakness, his poorness, his humbleness at this time.   I knew that six times we had repulsed his forces: thrice in Ireland; thrice at sea,—once upon our coast, twice upon his own.   Thrice had I served against him myself at sea, wherein for

my country's sake I had expended of my own
property forty thousand marks. I knew that
where beforetimes he was wont to have forty
great sails, at the least, in his ports, now he hath
not past six or seven. And for sending to his
Indies he was driven to have strange vessels, a
thing contrary to the institutions of his ancestors,
who straitly forbade that, even in case of necessity, they should make their necessity known to
strangers. I knew that, of twenty-five millions
which he had from his Indies, he had scarce any
left. Nay, I knew his poorness to be such at this
time as [that] the Jesuits, his imps, begged at his
church doors. [I knew] his pride so abated that,
notwithstanding his former high terms, he was
glad to congratulate his majesty, and send unto
him. Whoso knew what great assurances were
required from other states, for smaller sums, would
not think he would so freely disburse to my Lord
Cobham six hundred thousand crowns! And, if
I had minded to set my Lord Cobham a-work in
such a case, I would have given him some instruc-
tions how to persuade the king. For I knew

Cobham no such minion that could persuade a
king that was in want to disburse so great a sum,
without great reason, and some assurance for his
money. I knew the Queen of England lent not
her money to the States, without she had Flushing, Brill, and other towns, in assurance for it.
She lent not money to the King of France, without she had Newhaven for it. Nay, her own
subjects, the merchants of London, did not lend
her money, without they had her lands in pawn
for it. And to show that I am not 'Spanish'—
as you term me—at this time I had writ a treatise
to the king's majesty of the present state of Spain,
and reasons against the peace.

"For my inwardness with the Lord Cobham,
it was only in matters of private estate, wherein,
he communicating often with me, I lent him my
best advice. At this time I was to deal with the
duke for him, to procure a fee farm from the
king; for which purpose I had about me in my
bosom, when I was first examined, four thousand
pounds worth of his jewels. He being a baron
of this realm, upon whom all the honors of his

house rested; his possessions great; having goodly houses, worth at least five thousand pounds a year revenue; his plate and furniture as rich as was any man of his rank,—is it likely I could so easily incite a man of these fortunes to enter into so gross treasons? And for further argument that he was not desperate in estate nor poor in purse, he offered four thousand pounds for this fee farm. Not three days before his apprehending he had bestowed one hundred and fifty pounds in books, which he sent to his house at Canterbury. He gave [too] three hundred pounds for a cabinet, which he offered to you, master attorney, for the drawing of his book. He had the value of thirty-five hundred pounds in one piece of [plate], besides one ring worth five hundred pounds; and besides many others jewels, of price. Think now if it be likely that this man, upon an idle humor, would venture all this. As for my knowing that he had conspired all these things with Spain, for Arabella, and against the king, I protest before Almighty God I am as clear as whosoever here is freest."

The next thing brought forward by the attorney general was the document which Cobham refused to sign at first, but was afterward constrained to do so by the Chief-Justice Popham saying that he would be compelled to do so.

The chief-justice then, contrary to all the rules of courts of justice, volunteers his testimony. "I came to the Lord Cobham, and told him he ought to subscribe, which presently after the Lord Cobham did. And he said of Sir Walter Raleigh in the doing of it, 'That wretch! That traitor Raleigh!' And surely the countenance and action of my Lord Cobham much satisfied me that what he had confessed was true, and that he surely thought that Sir Walter had betrayed him."

What a procedure for a judge upon the bench trying the case! The foreman of the jury asked for the time of Lord Cobham's accusation. Lord Cecil then, half apologizing for testifying in Raleigh's favor, answered that Raleigh was examined at the outset of the inquiry, and that he testified nothing against Lord Cobham whatsoever.

Cobham was deceived, and was so enraged against Raleigh that he accused him of treason.

Coke then replied at length to Raleigh's speech, after which Raleigh begged to have his accuser brought face to face to him, and declared that to rely on one witness in such a case was contrary to the law of God and the justice of mankind.

Both the justices decided that it was according to law and usage, and they denied his right to demand the presence of his accuser.

The matter of Raleigh's receiving a part of the money expected of the King of Spain was then brought in. To this Raleigh made the following reply:

" Mr. Attorney, you have seemed to say much, but in truth nothing that applies to me. You conclude that I must know of the plot because I was to have a part of the money. But all you have said concerning this I have made void by distinguishing the time when it was spoken. It is true, my Lord Cobham had speech with me about the money, and made me an offer. But how? and when? Voluntarily; one day at dinner, sometime before Count Aremberg's coming over. For he and I, being at his own board, arguing and speaking violently—he for the peace, I against the peace, the Lord Cobham told me that when Count Aremberg came, he would give such strong arguments for the peace as would satisfy any man. And withal he told, as his fashion is to utter things easily, what great sums of money would be given to some councilors for making the peace, and he named my Lord Cecil and the Earl of Mar. I answering, bade him make no such offer to them, for they would hate him if he did offer it. Now, if often thus my Lord Cobham changed his mind as to the use to be made of the money, and joining with Lord Grey and the others, had any such treasonable intent as is alleged, *what is that to me?* They must answer it, not I. The offer of the money to me is nothing, for it was made before Count Aremberg's coming. The offer made to others was afterward."

Lord Henry Howard said: "Allege me any ground or cause why you gave ear to my Lord

Cobham on receiving of pensions in matters you had not to deal in."

Raleigh replied: "Could I stop my Lord Cobham's mouth?"

Cecil then appealed to the judges to say whether the accuser of Raleigh should not be brought face to face with accused.

Justices Popham and Gowdy denied the right of the prisoner to claim this by law.

The examinations of Capley and of Raleigh were then read, in which Raleigh was charged with saying that "the way to invade England was to begin with stirs in Scotland."

Raleigh replied: "I think so still. I have spoken it often to divers of the lords by way of discourse and my opinion."

Coke then said: "Now let us come to the words of destroying of 'the king and his cubs.'"

Raleigh exclaimed: "Oh, barbarous! If they, like unnatural villains, spoke such words, shall I be charged with them? I will not hear it. I was never false to the crown of England. I have spent forty thousand pounds of mine own against the Spanish faction for the good of my country. Do you bring the words of those hellish spiders Clarke, Watson, and others against me?"

Coke retorted: "Thou hast a Spanish heart, and thyself art a spider of hell. For thou confessest the king to be a most sweet and gracious prince, and yet thou hast conspired against him."

The only proof of this allegation was that Brooke stated in his examination that he thought that the project of "the destruction of the king was infused into his brother's head by Raleigh."

"If this may be," exclaimed Raleigh, indignantly protesting against such evidence, "you will have any man's life in a week!"

It was then read from Cobham's examination: "I had from Raleigh a book written against the title of the king. I gave it to my brother. Raleigh said, 'It was foolishly written.'"

Raleigh replied to this: "I never gave it him. He took it off my table. For I remember a little before that time I received a challenge from Sir Amias Preston, and for that I did resolve to answer it. I resolved to leave my estate settled, and, therefor, laid out all my loose papers, amongst which was this book."

The point which was then made was whether this book was given to Cobham before or after the Lord Cobham was known to be discontented with King James. As to the matter of it, Lord Henry Howard testified that Cobham had contradicted himself on this subject, having first said it was against the king's title, and afterward said that "it contained nothing against the king's title, and that he had it not from Sir Walter Raleigh, but took it from his table when he was sleeping."

Various other matters were now introduced and discussed; but as they had no vital bearing upon the case, it would be tedious to describe them.

Raleigh repeatedly insisted that the only important witness against him should be produced in court. The final dispute about this is thus described by Edwards:

Coke. "He is a party, and may not come. The law is against it."

Raleigh. "It is a toy to tell me of law. I defy law. I stand on the facts."

Lord Cecil. "I am afraid my plain speech, who am inferior to my lords here in presence, will make the world think I delight to hear myself talk. My affection to you, Sir Walter Raleigh, has not extinguished, but slacked, in regard of your defects. You know the reason, to which your mind doth not contest, that my Lord Cobham can not be brought."

Raleigh. "He may be, my lord."

Lord Cecil. "But dare you challenge it?"

Raleigh. "Now."

Attorney General Coke. "You say that my Lord Cobham, your main accuser, must come to accuse you. You say that he hath retracted. What the validity of all this is, is merely left to the jury. Let me only ask you this: If my Lord Cobham will say that you are the only instigator of him to proceed in the treason, dare you put yourself on this?"

Raleigh. "If he will speak it before God and the king, that even I knew of Arabella's matter for the money out of Spain, or of the 'surprising treason,' I put myself on it. God's will and the king's be done with me."

Lord Henry Howard. "How if he speak things equivalent to what you have said?"

Raleigh. "Yes, in a main point."

Lord Cecil. "If he say you have been the instigator of him to deal with the Spanish king, had not the council cause to draw you hither?"

Raleigh. "I put myself on it."

Lord Cecil. "Then call to God, Sir Walter, and prepare yourself; for I do verily believe my lord will prove this. Excepting your fault, I am your friend. The great passion in you, and the attorney's zeal for the king's service, make me speak thus."

Raleigh. "Whosoever is the workman, it is reason he should give account of his work to the work-master. But let it be proved that he acquainted me with any of his conference with Aremberg."

Lord Cecil. "That follows not. If I set you a

work, and you give me no account, am I therefore innocent?"

Coke. "For Arabella, I have said that she was never acquainted with the matter. Now, that Raleigh hath had conference in all these treasons it is manifest. The jury hath heard out the matter. There is one Dyer, a pilot, that, being in Lisbon, met with a Portuguese gentleman, who asked him if the King of England was crowned yet. To whom he answered, 'I think not yet, but he shall be shortly.' 'Nay,' saith the Portuguese, 'that shall never be, for his throat will be cut by Don Raleigh and Don Cobham, before he be crowned.'"

Hereupon Dyer was called. He deposed upon oath to the hearing of these words in a conversation at Lisbon.

Raleigh. "What inference upon that?"

Coke. "That your treason hath wings."

Raleigh. "If Cobham did practice with Aremberg, how could it not be known in Spain? Why did they name the Duke of Bucks with Jack Straw? It was to countenance his treasons."

And so the trial went on. At length Cobham's letter to the lords was read to the court. He begins by saying that he read two letters from Raleigh in the Tower. To the first he made no answer; to the second he replied out of pity to his wife and children, and because he was put in hope of the proceedings against him being staid. "With the like truth," he goes on to say, "I will proceed to tell you my dealings toward Count Aremberg to get him (that is, Raleigh,) a pension of *one thousand five hundred pounds per annum* for intelligence, and he would always tell and advertise what was intended against Spain, for the Low Countries, or with France. And coming from Greenwich one night, he acquainted me with what was agreed betwixt the king and the Low Countrymen, that I should impart it to Count Aremberg. But upon this motion for *one thousand five hundred pounds per annum* for intelligence, I never dealt with Count Aremberg. Now, as by this may appear to your lordships, he hath been the original cause of my ruin. For, but by his instigation, I had never dealt

with Count Aremberg.   And so he hath been
the only cause of my discontentment; I never
coming from the Count, but still he filled and
possessed me with new causes of discontentment.
To conclude: in his last letter he advised me
that I should not be overtaken by confessing to
any particular, for the king would better allow
my constant denial than my after-appealing.   For
my after-accusing would but add matter to my
former offense."

Several times the reading of this confession
and accusation was interrupted by taunting ex-
clamations, such: "Is not this a Spanish heart
in an English body!"   At the close he demanded
of Raleigh: "What say you now to the letter?"

"I say," said Raleigh, "that Cobham is a
base, dishonorable, poor soul."

"Is he base?" said Coke.   "I return it into
their own throat in his behalf.   But for them he
had been a good subject."

The best report of the trial puts the following
in the mouth of Sir Walter:

"I pray you, hear me in a word, and you

12

shall see how many souls this Cobham hath. And the king shall judge by one death which of us is the perfidious man. Before my Lord Cobham's coming from the Tower, I was advised by some of my friends to get a confession from him. Therefor I wrote to him thus: 'You or I must go to trial. If I first, then your accusation is the only evidence against me.' It was not ill of me to beg him to say the truth. But his first letter was not to my contenting. I writ a second, and then he writ me a very good letter. But I sent him word I feared Mr. Lieutenant of the Tower might be blamed if it was discovered that letters had passed. Though I protest, Sir George Harvey is not to blame, for what passed. No keeper in the world could so provide but it might happen. So I sent him the letter again with this: 'It is likely now that you shall be the first tried.' But the Lord Cobham sent to me again: 'It is not unfit you had such a letter.' And here you may see it, and, I pray you, read it." And with this he presented the letter.

Lord Cecil, as being familiar with Cobham's

handwriting, was requested by Raleigh to read the letter aloud.

"Now that the arraignment draws near, not knowing which shall be first, I or you, to clear my conscience, satisfy the world, and free myself from the cry of your blood, I protest upon my soul and before God and his angels, I never had conference with you in any treason, nor was ever moved by you to the things I heretofore accused you of. And for any thing I know, you are as innocent and as clear of any treason against the king as is any subject living. Therefore I wash my hands, and pronounce '*Purus sum a sanguine hujus.*' And so God deal with me, and have mercy on my soul, as this is true."

This being read, Sir Walter rose, and said:

"Now, my masters, you have heard both. That shewed against me is but a voluntary confession; this is under oath and the deepest protestations a Christian can make. Therefore believe which of these hath the most force."

There the case ended. The jury retired as usual to make up their verdict. To the surprise of every body, they returned in a quarter of an hour, and brought in a verdict of "guilty of treason." It was evident that they had acted from prejudice rather than judgment, for the case was to every reflecting and candid mind one of no ordinary difficulty. Sir Walter had not been wholly without complicity in Cobham's transactions; but he had not been guilty of treason, nor even of misprision of treason. Coke himself was surprised by the verdict. He had walked out into the garden when the jury retired, and when the verdict was mentioned to him, he declared his astonishment, for he had not really meant to charge him with any thing more than "*misprision of treason*." One writer reports that several of the jury were "so touched in their conscience" that they came afterward to Sir Walter, and on their knees confessed their injustice, and begged his pardon. Mrs. Thompson thinks that this is not likely, "since the men who gave such a verdict must either have been compelled by fear or induced by bribery to compromise their sense of justice, and either of these motives would have kept them silent after their decision." The prisoner received the verdict coolly. Upon being asked, according to the forms of law, what he had to say why sentence should not be pronounced upon him, he rose, and said:

"My lords, the jury hath found me guilty. They must do as they are directed. I can say nothing why judgment should not proceed. You see whereof Cobham hath accused me. You remember his protestation that I was never guilty. I desire the king should know the wrong I have been subject to since I came hither."

The chief-justice said: "You have had no wrong, Sir Walter."

"Yes," said Raleigh of the attorney, "I desire the lords to remember these things to the king. I was accused to be a practicer with Spain. I never knew that Lord Cobham meant to go thither. I will ask no mercy at the king's hands if he will affirm it. Secondly, I never knew of the practices with Arabella. Thirdly, I never knew of my Lord Cobham's practice with Aremberg, nor of the 'surprising' treason."

The chief-justice then made a long and abusive speech, blaming Raleigh's not confessing any thing as an inhuman and wicked conceit, and closing with sentencing him to be hanged and afterward beheaded. Raleigh then turned to the Earl of Devonshire and other lords, and solicited their influence with the king to change the mode of his death to one less ignominious. He also approached Cecil and the lay commissioners, and asked them to have Cobham brought first to the scaffold, and made to confront him. "He is a false and cowardly accuser. He can face neither me nor death without acknowledging his false-hood." He was then conducted back to the castle to await the final decision of the king as to the execution of the sentence.

Sir Roger Orton, a Scotchman in the service of the king, brought him the news of Raleigh's condemnation. He could not help saying that "never had man spoken so well in times past, nor would do so in times to come." Another Scotchman, who accompanied Sir Roger to the king, declared for himself, "that, although he would before his trial have gone a thousand miles to see him hanged, he would, ere he parted, have gone a thousand miles to have saved his life." This honest remark expresses the feeling of most of the spectators of the trial. At one time Coke was hissed as he uttered his coarse abuse; and Raleigh's noble bearing under provocation and pathetic appeals to the jury so deeply affected the audience and revolutionized their feelings, that one present remarked, "Never was a man so hated and so popular in so short a time."

The trial of Cobham came next in order. The reading of the indictment was interrupted by his occasional denial of several particulars, and he charged Raleigh with exciting discontent in his mind, but denied any treasonable intentions. He admitted the truth of his first confession, and made a merit of it, and a plea for pardon. When asked about his contradictory letters respecting Raleigh's complicity in his crime, he affirmed the truth of the first letter, in which he condemned Raleigh. The trial occupied but little time, and he was pronounced guilty of treason.

Chapter XV.

EXECUTION OF THE PRISONERS WATSON, CLARKE, AND
BROOKE—THE KING'S MANEUVERS IN REGARD TO THE
FATE OF RALEIGH, COBHAM, GREY, AND MARKHAM.

EARLY in December, 1603, the authors of
the "surprise" plots, Watson, Clarke, and
Brooke, were executed at Winchester. They
were hung until nearly dead, then cut down and
beheaded, then drawn and quartered, according
to the barbaric usage of those times. Clarke
justified the part he had taken in the movement,
but Watson confessed his guilt, and acknowledged the justice of his punishment. Brooke
spoke mysteriously of some hidden cause of his
course of conduct, saying with his last breath:
"There is somewhat hidden that will one day
appear for my justification." This statement produced much alarm at first among the courtiers;
but nothing appeared to explain it, and the sen-

sation passed away. While in prison he confessed to the bishop who administered to him the
last sacrament that he had falsely accused his
brother and Sir Walter Raleigh.

While waiting in prison the time appointed for
his execution, Raleigh's friends made the most
earnest exertions to procure his pardon from the
king. The beloved wife of Raleigh wrote to
Cecil, and visited him, and on her knees entreated his influence in favor of her husband.
The Countess of Pembroke entreated her son as
he valued a mother's blessing to exert himself in
every possible way to save the life of Sir Walter.
The lords of the council who had judged him
united in petitioning the king to show mercy
in this beginning of his reign, and to "gain the
title of Clemens as well as of Justus." Sir Walter
himself wrote letters to the king and to the lords
of the council, begging for his life in terms so
humble and even abject, that he afterward was
ashamed of it, and wrote to his wife, "Get those
letters, if it be possible, which I wrote to the
lords, wherein I sued for life. God knows it was

for you and yours that I desired it. But it is true that I disdain myself for begging it."

Queen Anne, and both the French and Spanish embassadors, besought the king to show mercy to the prisoners, and even bribes were given to leading politicians, according to the corrupt usage of the age, to purchase their interposition.

But no word or sign came from the king to inspire hope. The clergymen who visited the prisoners in the exercise of their spiritual functions, were instructed to prepare them for death. One of the king's chaplains, preaching at Wilton before the king and court, declared that clemency to traitors was a sin against God and the state. He could not have done a better thing to induce James to exercise the mercy he deprecated, for he loved to show himself independent and self-moved in all his official acts. He went from the chapel, and wrote a warrant to stay the execution; but he kept it in his own hands. The next day he signed the death warrants of Markham, Grey, and Cobham, and sent them to the sheriff at Winchester, to be executed two days after that,

Friday, December 10, 1603, the day fixed for the execution.   Raleigh's execution was fixed for Monday, the 13th of December.

Markham was first brought forward for execution.   He had cherished hopes of a reprieve or pardon, but the day before his advices extinguished them altogether, and he appeared on the scaffold deeply distressed in mind, but undaunted.   A friend offered him a napkin, to conceal his face, but he declined it, saying, "I can look upon death without blushing."   He said that he had been so led to cherish hopes of pardon that he had not given sufficient attention to preparing himself for death. but now he bade his friends adieu, and, having knelt for some time in prayer, he prepared himself for the executioner.

As Raleigh looked from the window of the prison, to witness the fate of those who were to precede him, he observed the sheriff to pause and turn toward a magistrate pushing his way through the crowd.   It was Sir James Hayes, who had received from a messenger a letter containing the king's warrant for a stay of execution.   The

sheriff then turned to the prisoner, standing over
the block, and said: "You say that you are not
prepared to die! You shall have two hours'
respite." He was then led from the scaffold into
a hall, called Arthur's Hall, and locked in by
himself, without any explanation of the mystery
of his reprieve. It was the conceit of the small-
minded king to punish the prisoners with the
terrors of death, and then to commute the sentence to imprisonment.

The next scene in this "comedy," as it has
been styled, was the appearance of Lord Grey,
who was brought forth by the sheriff to go through
the same experience, without knowing what had
happened. The young and popular nobleman
was surrounded by friends, who came to cheer
his last moments; and he appeared like one going
to his marriage, rather than to his execution. He
made a long prayer, in which he protested to
God his innocence of treason, but confessed that
he deserved to die for his plotting against the
king. The sheriff waited for him to finish his
prayer, and then stepped up to him and, to his

surprise, told him that the king had sent word that Cobham should precede him, and that he was to wait for a time. He was then conducted into Arthur's Hall, where, to his astonishment, he found Markham.

Cobham now appeared, attended by a minister. He showed no dismay at the prospect of death, but he repeated the prayers of the minister with special earnestness. He then expressed sorrow for his offense, and reiterated his accusation of Raleigh, saying, "It is true, as I have hope of my soul's resurrection." He was then told that he was, by the king's orders, to be confronted with some other prisoners.

Presently the sheriff had Grey and Markham brought out and placed before him. He then addressed the group: "Are not your offenses grievous? Have you not been justly tried and condemned? Is not each of you subject to due execution, now to be performed?" The prisoners assented to the accusations. "Now, then," said the sheriff, "see the mercy of your prince, who of himself hath sent hither a countermand, and

hath given you your lives!" Upon this being
announced, the crowd about the scaffold ap·
plauded long and lustily. The sentence of death
was commuted to imprisonment for life, or during
the pleasure of the king.

At the court in Wilton the king, as a part of
this comic tragedy, addressed his courtiers on the
crimes and characters of the prisoners, and con·
cluded by saying that, as he could not show
mercy to one without partiality, he concluded
to "save the lives of them all."

Sir Walter Raleigh, for some reason, was
spared the ignominy and agony of this mock
execution. He remained at Winchester a month,
and was then returned to the Tower, under the
guard of Sir William Wade. Sir George Harvey
was still the lieutenant of the Tower, and held
the office until August, 1605. This officer seems
to have treated his prisoner with all proper respect and kindness. He was not shut up, as a
recent historian pictures, in a cell ten feet by
eight, without even a window to let in the light
of day; but he had a decent chamber, open to

the garden of the lieutenant, of which he had the
freedom, at least during the day. He was allowed
the company of his wife and son, young Walter;
also the frequent attendance of his servants, the
visits of his physicians, and of his clerical friend,
Rev. Gilbert Hawthorne. He had permission
occasionally to visit the cells of other prisoners,
and especially Cobham's apartment, near by. He
had the use of his library, and he constructed a
rude chemical laboratory out of the hen-house in
the garden, where he spent much of his time in
experiments, and, it is said, obtained some celeb-
rity for various nostrums invented by him.

One of his nostrums was like to have involved
him in trouble. One day the Countess of Beaumont made a visit to the Tower, and, among
other places, called at the garden, and asked Sir
Walter to furnish her with some of his "Balsam
of Guiana." This was sent to her by one Captain
Whitlocke, who was seen in her train that day.
This gentleman was a retainer of the Earl of
Northumberland, who was afterward connected
with the Gunpowder Plot; and this circumstance

gave rise to a suspicion that Sir Walter was knowing to that conspiracy. He was brought before the lords and examined, but was acquitted.

Besides his favorite recreations, music and painting, he devoted his time to reading and writing. The most important of all his productions during his long imprisonment was the " History of the World." A part of this was published 1604. The second volume, in a fit of passion, he destroyed. One day his publisher, Walter Burse, was asked how the work sold. He answered, "So slowly that it has undone me." Whereupon Sir Walter, taking the second volume from the shelf, said, "The second volume shall undo ye no more; this ungrateful world is unworthy of it." He then threw it into the fire. "Both in style and matter," says a writer in Chambers's Encyclopœdia, "this celebrated work is vastly superior to all the English historical productions which had previously appeared. Its style, though partaking of the faults of the age, in being frequently stiff and inverted, has less of those defects than the diction of any other writer of the time. Mr. Tytler with justice commends it as vigorous, purely English, and possessing an antique richness of ornament, similar to what pleases us when we see some ancient priory or stately manor-mansion, and compare it with our more modern mansions. The work is laborious without being heavy, learned without being dry, acute and ingenious without degener-ating into the subtle but trivial distinctions of the schoolmen. Its narration is clear and spirited, and the matter collected from the most authentic sources. The opinions of the author upon state policy, on the causes of great events, on the dif-ferent forms of government, on naval and military tactics, on agriculture, commerce, manufactures, and other sources of national greatness, are not the mere echo of other minds, but the results of experience drawn from the study of a long life, spent in constant action and vicissitude, in vari-ous climates and countries, and from personal labor in offices of high trust and responsibility. But perhaps its most striking feature is the sweet tone of philosophic melancholy which pervades the whole. Written in prison during the quiet evening of a tempestuous life, we feel in its perusal that we are the companions of a superior mind, nursed in contemplation and chastened and improved by sorrow, in which the bitter recollections of injury and the asperity of resentment have passed away, leaving only the heavenly lesson that all is vanity."

Why this valuable and eloquent history did not sell can not be explained. It shared the fate of many other productions of genius which contemporaries have left to after times to appreciate.

Besides this, Raleigh composed treatises entitled: "Discourses on the Match with Savoy;" "Treatise on the Art of War by Sea, Ancient and Modern;" "Discourses of the Invention of Ships;" "Observations Concerning the Royal Navy." The first of this list was written by the request of Prince Henry, the heir-apparent of the English throne, on the occasion of the Spanish embassador proposing to the king to marry his daughter to the eldest son of the Duke of Savoy, and his son, Prince Henry, to a daughter of the same prince. Raleigh gave good and substantial reasons why this twofold match should not be made; and by so doing he incurred the displeasure of the king and some of his advisers. He forfeited also some of his privileges at the Tower; and was placed under close imprisonment for three months. Prince Henry, however, was his fast friend, and gave every encouragement to his literary labors.

Such was Sir Walter's condition for twelve long, weary years. As to the other prisoners, Lord Grey died in the Tower in 1614; and Cobham, after remaining about the same length of time in prison, was set at liberty, to pass a few more wretched years in poverty, neglect, and disgrace, and to die in a garret. While yet in prison, he confessed the falsity of his accusation of Raleigh, when Queen Anne contrived to have him examined again under oath. He lived long enough to see the sad doom of his victim, and soon after passed to his account before the Great Judge. As it respects Markham, the author has no knowledge of what happened to him after his removal to the Tower.

Chapter XVI.

DEATH OF CECIL AND PRINCE HENRY—RALEIGH RELEASED
FROM THE TOWER—PROJECTS ANOTHER
EXPEDITION TO GUIANA.

ROBERT CECIL, Lord Treasurer of the
Government of James I, was the second
son of William Cecil, Lord Burleigh, the wise and
successful leader of the previous reign. He was
of a delicate and somewhat deformed frame, but
with a mind keen, alert, and fruitful. He grad-
uated at the Cambridge University. His first important office under the government of Elizabeth
was as assistant to the embassador to France,
Lord Derby. In 1596 he was made one of the
secretaries of state, and finally he became the
principal secretary and privy councilor to the
queen. He secretly favored the claim of James
to the succession. One day, traveling with the
queen, he received dispatches from the Scottish

court, and upon being asked about it by her, he pretended that it pertained to some of his private affairs, and eluded her vigilance. On the accession of James he was continued in his office. Though in person he was not such as the weak-minded king liked to have around him, the charms of his eloquence, his penetrating and comprehensive intellect, and the substantial integrity of his moral character won for him the royal confidence. He was successively made a baron, Viscount of Cranbourn, and Earl of Salisbury. He was chosen chancellor of Cambridge University, and in 1608 lord high treasurer. He was a friend of Raleigh when Sir Walter was the favorite of Elizabeth, and he always pretended to be, though he took the part of the king in his disgrace and condemnation. He was in religious sentiment inclined to Puritanism. In 1612 his health gave way, and on his journey to London from Bath, where he had in vain sought relief in its mineral springs from complicated diseases, he died at Marlborough on the 28th of May. He welcomed death as the great release from care and trouble. "Ease and pleasure quake to hear of death," he said; "but my life, full of cares and miseries, desireth to be dissolved." His last hours were employed in devotion, and such was his expression of hope and trust in the Redeemer that it shed around his dying bed on the minds of all who attended him a twilight of immortality.

The death of Cecil removed one obstacle to the pardon and release of Raleigh, for he believed that the judgment against him was just, and so advised the king not to accede to the petitions of distinguished friends, including Queen Anne, who were interested in his favor. Only six months after this event the death of Raleigh's friend, Prince Henry, brought a deeper cloud over his prospects. This young man possessed superior qualities of mind and heart. He was the idol of his mother; but his father's heart was made cold toward him by the difference of their views in regard to matters of state policy, and by his growing popularity. Early in the Fall he began to complain of giddiness in the head, attended with pain. He resorted as a remedy to traveling about from place to place; but without success. Drowsiness and coldness in the head and the pallor of his countenance indicated that his end was approaching.   On his last appearing at public worship, the text was ominous of his destiny: "Man that is born of a woman is of few days and full of trouble · he cometh forth like a flower, and is cut down: he fleeth also as a shadow, and continueth not." (Job xiv, 1, 2.)   Some weeks before his death he went down to Woolwich to witness, in company with his mother, the launching of a ship built for him on a plan suggested by Raleigh, and called after him "*The Prince.*" The launch was not successful at the first; but subsequent trials sent her forth on her mission. And she was destined to do a good service for the royal family, for it was in that ship Prince Charles outrode the fearful gale which swept many feeble craft to destruction.

As Prince Henry drew near his end, Raleigh was applied to by the queen for a cordial he had invented in the Tower, and which had given her relief in a severe illness, and had a great reputa-

tion and run in the land. Raleigh sent it with
the remark that it would cure the prince or any
one of a fever if not poisoned. Such was the
credulity of those times in respect to the efficacy
of specific doses. But the disease of the prince
had too far progressed for any earthly relief. All
the effect it had was to soothe his sufferings and
procure sleep. The queen was compelled to
witness the death of her noble son, and she believed to her dying day that he was the victim
of poison. Various stories were circulated; some
said that he was poisoned by a bunch of grapes,
some by poisoned gloves. His chaplain hesitated not to declare his belief in the truth of
these rumors. Suspicion fell upon Robert Car,
Viscount Rochester, the king's favorite, upon the
Spaniards, the Catholics, and even upon King
James himself. The queen believed that Car
was the instigator of his death, and refused
to see him ever after. That he was capable of
so great a crime was proved by his poisoning
two years afterward the food of Sir Thomas Over-
bury in the Tower, as was proved by the apothe-

cary's clerk who prepared the last fatal dose for the unhappy prisoner.

The death of Prince Henry put an end to Sir Walter's expectation of a speedy release from the Tower. That brave and amiable youth had ventured to urge this favor with his eccentric father, and had prevailed so far as to get the promise of it by the next Christmas; but the merry bells of Christmas were sounded over his grave, and the promise of the king was buried with him. The queen remained his friend, and in 1614 her intercessions on the plea of Raleigh's failing health in confinement procured for him the liberty of the Tower, that is, permission to go about it for recreation without leaving its walls.

During this year he was afflicted by the flight of his son Walter to Netherlands, to avoid the consequences of a duel he had with Robert Tyrwhit, an attaché of the Earl of Suffolk, then the lord high treasurer succeeding Cecil. The affair blew over soon, and Walter returned to England.

The time was now at hand when Raleigh was to once more enjoy liberty and the privilege of

serving his country. The unprincipled Car was
succeeded as favorite of the king by George
Villiers, afterward Duke of Buckingham. To
this young man as gentleman of the bed-chamber,
having the ear of the king, Raleigh made overtures for his liberation. These he backed up by
the influence of the mother of Villiers, and by
his uncles, Sir William and Sir Edward, whose
efforts he purchased, according to the corrupt
custom of the times, by the payment of one
thousand five hundred pounds. He had also
favorably impressed the king's ministers, especially Sir Ralph Winwood, Secretary of State,
with his project of a second expedition to Guiana.
He had during his imprisonment sent a vessel
every year to Guiana to assure the natives of the
favor and protection of the English against the
Spanish colonies. He believed he was doing a
great service to the king, and he longed to be
free to show his loyalty by such "service as had
seldom been performed for any king." The long-
desired order for his liberation was sent by the
king on the 30th of January, 1616. He was al-

lowed to reside at his own house, but was under the surveillance of a keeper. On the 19th of March the privy council wrote to him, giving permission to undertake measures for the Guiana expedition in the following terms:

"His majesty, out of his gracious inclinations toward you, being pleased to release you out of your imprisonment in the Tower to go abroad with a keeper to make your provisions for your intended voyage, we think it good to admonish you (though we do not prejudicate your own discretion so much as to think you would attempt it without leave) that you should not presume to resort either to his majesty's court, the queen's, or prince's, nor go into any public assemblies wheresoever, without especial license obtained from his majesty for your warrant. But only that you use the benefit of his majesty's grace to follow the business which you are to undertake, and for which, upon your humble request, his majesty hath been graciously pleased to grant you that pardon."

Was ever a condemned criminal before or

since employed by any government to take charge
of an important enterprise for the benefit of the
nation before pardon had been given him, and
while he was under the oversight of a keeper?
Just such was the intolerable meanness of King
James. His purpose was to let this great adven-
turer make an experiment to find the gold mines
of South America. If he succeeded, the king
would be made rich; if he did not succeed, he
should lose his head. Sir Walter was anxious
about getting his pardon before he set forth, and
consulted with Lord Bacon in regard to it; but
Bacon assured him that it was not necessary, for
pardon was implied in his appointment as admiral of the fleet and commander of the expedition. Time will show how this was understood
by the king.

Before Raleigh left the Tower, two events took
place of deepest interest to him—the death of
Lady Arabella Stuart and the imprisonment of
Robert Car, Earl of Somerset, to whom the king
had given Sherborne, the forfeited estate of Raleigh, saying to those who objected, "I maun

have it for Car." "The whole history of the world," said Raleigh, "had not a like precedent of a king's prisoner to purchase freedom, and his bosom favorite to have the halter, but in Scripture, in the case of Mordecai and Haman." As to poor Lady Arabella, whose only crime was that she had royal blood in her veins, being the granddaughter of Henry VII, and next to James in the line of succession to the throne of England, she was not proved to have any participation in the conspiracy of Cobham and others to place her on the throne, and was left at liberty. But subsequently it was discovered that she had secretly married the grandson of the Earl of Hertford, and for that she and her husband were sent to the Tower. In the course of the year they escaped; but Arabella was captured, and taken back to prison. These troubles wrought upon her mind, and deprived her of her reason. At her death, in September, 1615, she was thirty-eight years of age.

Chapter XVII.

THE GUIANA EXPEDITION.

WITH characteristic alacrity and devotion to business, Sir Walter Raleigh began his preparations for the voyage. For this purpose he called in a loan of eight thousand pounds to the Countess of Bedford, and added two thousand five hundred pounds from the sale of Lady Raleigh's estate at Mitcham in Surrey, which she freely contributed for her husband's sake. His friends, among whom were the Earls of Huntingdon and Arundel, and some merchants, chiefly foreigners, took shares in the enterprise; but no pecuniary aid was given by the government. A commission was given, August 26, 1616, to Sir Walter, constituting him admiral of the fleet. Authority was given him "to carry for the voyage to Guiana so many of the British subjects as should willingly accompany him, with an

unlimited supply of arms, ammunition, ships, etc."
Also to trade with the natives, and to bring home
gold, silver, etc., "for the proper use of Sir
Walter Raleigh and his company, reserving to
the king and his heirs one-fifth only of such im-
portations." Raleigh was also constituted general
and commander of the enterprise, governor of the
new country, with the privilege of exercising
martial law, in a similar manner to the county
lieutenants of England, or to the lieutenant-general of land or sea forces. It is said that the
document began in the usual way, with the
words, "To our trusty and well beloved knight,
Sir Walter Raleigh;" and it was pleaded afterward that these words implied a pardon from
the king.

On the 28th of March, 1618, the fleet was
ready to sail. It consisted of seven vessels as it
proceeded down the Thames, and at Plymouth it
was joined by four more, making eleven sail.
Walter Raleigh, Jr., was made captain of the flag-
ship, the *Destiny*. The other captains were, Sir
John Ferne, Lawrence Keymis, Wallaston, Chad-

leigh, and Pennington. A carvel and two flyboats were added to the fleet at Plymouth. The
admiral's flag-ship was four hundred and fifty tons
burden, and carried thirty-six guns. Besides the
crew, there were on board two hundred volunteers, eighty of whom were gentlemen. A large
part of the company in the different ships were
of a low and dissolute character, whose native
land furnished them no prospect of success, and
whose friends were only too glad to get rid of
them, "at the hazard," as Raleigh said, "of some
thirty, forty, or sixty pounds, knowing that they
could not live so cheaply at home." To this
mixed company Raleigh published his Orders,
which a contemporary writer described as admirable, "fit to be written and engraven in every
man's soul that covets to do honor to his king
and country." Among the regulations was a
requisite of morning and evening worship, to be
omitted only in foul weather, when a psalm should
be sung at the setting of the evening watch. He
reminded his followers that " no enterprise can
prosper, be it by land or sea, without the favor

and assistance of Almighty God, the Lord and Strength of hosts and armies."

· The prayers and good wishes of numerous friends attended the departure of the fleet; but some friends prophesied evil would come to it. They knew that he had undertaken it from a desire to conciliate the king, more than from any spirit of enterprise, and they could not suppress the foreboding of disappointment.

Sylvanus Scory sent him, from London, the following lines, to cheer and assure him:

"Raleigh, in this thyself thyself transcends,
    When hourly tasting of a bitter chalice,
Scanning the sad faces of thy friends,
    Thou smil'st at Fortune's menaces and malice.

Hold thee firm here: cast anchor in this port:
    Here art thou safe till Death enfranchise thee:
Where neither harm, nor fears of harm, resort:
    Here, though enchained, thou liv'st in liberty.

Nothing on earth hath permanent abode,
    Nothing shall languish under sorrow still.
The Fates have set a certain period,
    As well to those that do as suffer ill."

The spectator who took the deepest interest in this enterprise was the Spanish embassador, Count

14

Gondomar. He felt that the success of Raleigh would be at the expense of Spain, and he had already contrived to impress King James with misgivings in regard to the propriety of the whole scheme. He had obtained from James a full catalogue of all the ships and of their armament, and had transmitted it to the Spanish court. It is clear, now, that Raleigh must succeed, or be ruined.

The fleet had scarcely got out of Plymouth Harbor, on the 12th of June, 1617, when a storm assailed them, and continued with violence for several weeks, and ended in a terrific tempest. They were then some eight leagues off the Scilly Islands. After the sinking of one vessel, the admiral signaled to the fleet to follow him to the harbor of Cork. Here for six weeks they were obliged to wait for a fair wind, a period long enough to have reached America, under favorable circumstances. This delay not only consumed precious time and provisions for the voyage, but gave rise to absurd rumors that he intended to turn pirate, and not to go on the Guiana expedition.

The first adventure that occurred after setting sail again was the chase and capture of four suspicious-looking ships, which were flying French colors. One of the shrewd captains of the fleet advised Raleigh not to credit their pretense of being merchantmen, but to confiscate them as corsairs. But he refused, saying, "It is no business of mine to examine the subjects of the French king." Some time afterward it turned out that he had proof that he was mistaken. They were pirates, and would have been lawful prey.

He reached the Canary Islands early in September, and came to anchor in Lancerota. The people were very much excited to see a fleet of thirteen vessels anchoring in their waters, taking them for Algerian pirates, as they had received warning of the intention of these ferocious corsairs to make their islands a visit. This suspicion was increased by some of the ships landing their crews in the night. But Raleigh sought an interview with the governor, and assured him of peaceable intentions, and asked leave to lay in water and provisions. The governor demanded that the crews should be recalled to the ships, as some conflict had already taken place between them and the natives, and three of the English had been wounded. Raleigh acceded to the request, much to the chagrin of some of his men, who wished to take vengeance on the town. But such conduct would have endangered the commerce of merchantmen with the islands, and have excited the displeasure of the king and the government.

One of his captains at this time proved himself a traitor. Bailey, captain of the *Husband*, stole away with his ship, and returned to England, where he reported that he left Sir Walter at Lancerota because he had landed in a hostile manner, and also meant to turn pirate. This man's conduct, it is suspected, was a part of a plot of his Spanish and English enemies at home to implicate Raleigh in unlawful transactions, and to bring ruin upon him.

Not having permission to purchase stores and to get supplies at the town, Raleigh moved down

the island, and landed some men to procure
water at an uninhabited place. But the ships
had been followed by hostile parties on shore,
and, while the seamen were busy filling their
casks, they were fired upon, and one of them
was killed. The assailants, numbering about
forty, were boldly attacked by young Walter Raleigh, at the head of a file of six or eight men,
and were driven from their ambush and scattered.

Proceeding thence, the fleet touched at Gomera, another of the Canaries. Here he received
a welcome quite in contrast with his recent experience. The wife of the governor was a noble
English lady; and on sending his message Raleigh
accompanied it with a present of English gloves.
He received in return from her a present of fruits,
rusks, and other needed refreshments, a part of
which he distributed among the sick men in the
fleet. He gave the strictest orders to his men to
avoid giving offense when on shore. The man
who should steal so much as an orange or a bunch
of grapes should be hung in the public square.
Before leaving the island, the governor expressed

his great gratification at the good behavior of the sailors, and even promised to send a letter to the same effect to the government at Madrid. His lady also sent on board a fresh store of fruit and poultry, in return for a present of lace, some perfumes prepared by Raleigh when in the Tower, and a beautiful picture of the Magdalen. "This incident," adds our eloquent authority, Edwards, "was to prove for a year to come the one pleasant oasis amid the dreary memories of a voyage crowded with calamity."

Leaving the Canaries, where his crew had been refreshed, and the sick among them improved in health or recovered, he encountered a series of disasters. The sickness which had been quelled broke out afresh in the fleet, and fifty men in his flag-ship were prostrated by it. Two captains, the chief surgeon, the provost marshal, and several other officers, died. Off the isle of Brava, one of the Cape de Verde Islands, in latitude 14° 48' north, and longitude 20° 44' west, one of the terrible hurricanes known to those tropical seas sunk one of his vessels, and damaged others.

The disease increased, until a large number of his
best men in all the ships were carried off, including John Pigott, the lieutenant-general of the land
forces, and his trusty servant John Talbot, his
assistant and companion in the Tower. Then
came calms more terrible than storms, with tor-
rents of rain that overwhelmed the ships and
filled the cabins.

So they fared until on the 11th of November
they sighted Cape Orange, then called Wiapoco;
and on the 14th they cast anchor in the river
Cayenne, then called Caliana. Here he made it
his first business to write the following letter to
his beloved and anxious wife:

"SWEETHEART,—I can yet write unto you but
with a weak hand, for I have suffered the most
violent calenture for fifteen days that ever man
did and lived; but God, that gave me a strong
heart in all my adversities, hath also now strengthened it in the hell-fire of heat.

"We have had two of the most grevious sick-
nesses in our ship, of which forty-two have died,
and there are yet many sick; but having recov-

ered the land of Guiana this 12th of November, I hope we shall recover them. We are yet two hundred men, and the rest of our fleet are reasonably strong—strong enough, I hope, to perform what we have undertaken, if the diligent care at London to make our strength known to the Spanish king by his embassador hath not taught the Spanish king to fortify all the entrances against us. Howsoever, we must make the adventure; and if we perish, it shall be no honor for England, nor gain for his majesty, to lose, among many others, one hundred as valiant gentlemen as England hath in it.

"Of Captain Bailey's base coming from us at the Canaries, see a letter of Kemish's to Mr. Scory; and of the unnatural weather, storms and rains and winds, he hath in the same letter given a touch. Of the way that hath been sailed in fourteen days, now hardly performed in forty days, God, I trust, will give us comfort in that which is to come. In the passage to the Canaries, I stayed at Gomera, where I took water in peace, because the country durst not deny it me. I received there of a countess of the English race a present of oranges, lemons, quinces, and pomegranates, without which I could not have lived. These I preserved in sands, and I have them yet to my great refreshing. Your son had never so good health, having no distemper in all the heat under the line. My servants have escaped but Crab and my cook; yet all have had the sickness. Crafts and March and the rest are all well. Remember my service to my Lord Carew and Mr. Secretary Winwood. I wrote not to them, for I can write of nothing but miseries yet.

"Of men of sort we have lost one sergeant-major, Captain Pigott, and his lieutenant, Captain Edward Hastings, who would have died at home, for both his liver, spleen, and brains were rotten; my son's lieutenant, Payton, and my cousin, Mr. Hews; Mr. Mordaunt, Mr. Gardiner, Mr. Hayward, Captain Jennings, the merchant; Kemish, of London, and the master chirurgeon; master refiner; Mr. Moor, the governor of Bermudas; our provost marshal, W. Steed; Lieutenant Vescie; but, to my inestimable grief, Hammon and Talbot.

By the next I trust you shall hear better of us. In God's hands we are, and in him we trust.

"This bearer, Captain Alley, for his infirmity of his head, I have sent back—an honest, valiant man. He can deliver you all that is past. Commend me to my worthy friends at Loathbury, Sir John Leigh, and Mr. Bower (whose nephew Knervit is well), and to my cousin Blundell, and my most devoted and humble service to his majesty.

"To tell you that I might be here king of the Indians were a vanity; but my name hath still lived among them. Here they feed me with fresh meat and all that the country yields. All offer to obey me. Commend me to poor Carew, my son.

"*From Calliana, in Guiana, the 14th of November*, 1617."

While these events were passing on this side the ocean, the deserter Bailey was doing his best in London to injure the reputation and destroy the influence of Sir Walter. He was called to an account for his conduct by the Lord Admiral Howard, the Earl of Nottingham, the former friend of Sir Walter in times gone by.

But when the case came before the privy council, the Lord Admiral was prevented from attending by sickness, and it happened, too, that Secretary Winwood, the friend of Raleigh in all these adventures, died suddenly, and not without suspicion that he had been poisoned. The result, therefore, of the inquiries was that the ship and goods which had been taken from Bailey were ordered to be restored to him, and he escaped the punishment due to his crimes. Not long after Captain Reeks, whose ship was in the harbor of Lancerota when Raleigh was there, and for whose sake in part he forbore to fire upon the town to avenge the treatment he had received of the governor and some of the people, arrived in England, and gave a true and unvarnished account of the affair. He said that at first the governor of the island had promised Sir Walter that "he should want for nothing the island afforded;" but afterward, without provocation, "all the goods of the town of Lancerota were sent to the mountains, and the governor sent Sir Walter Raleigh word that he was a pirate, and should have no more than what he could win by his sword." The effect of this testimony was to assure the friends of Raleigh, and to cause the arrest of Bailey, and his commitment to the State-house at Westminster.

To return to America, we find Sir Walter too ill to leave his ship, except as he was carried ashore in a chair. He makes inquiry for his friend Harry, the Indian who had so long looked for his return, and earnestly inquired after him of every English ship that had appeared on that coast. It was not long before Harry made his appearance, preceded and accompanied with munificent presents of "roasted mullets (which were very good meat), great store of plantains and pineapples, with pistachios (or ground-nuts), and divers other sorts of fruit."

The ships having taken time for needful repairs, orders were given to proceed toward the river Orinoco, and the "Triangle Isles" were made the "general *rendezvous*." Captain Keymis, who had familiar acquaintance with country, had the command of the expedition to search for the gold mines, the grand object of the whole enterprise. The land forces were placed under the general command of George Raleigh, the nephew of Sir Walter. Under him were Captains Raleigh, the son of Sir Walter, Parker, North. Thornhurst, and Hall.

Sir Walter, still suffering from a relapse of his disease, gave written directions to the principal commanders how to proceed. The land forces were to encamp "between the Spanish town and the mine, if there be any camp near it; that, being so secured, you may make trial what depth and breadth the mine holds, and whether or no it answers our hopes. If you find it royal, and the Spaniards begin to war on you, you, George Raleigh, are to repel them, if it be in your power, and to drive them as far as you can."

To Keymis he wrote: "If you find the mine be not so rich as may persuade the holding of it, and draw on a second supply, then you shall bring but a packet or two, to satisfy His Majesty that my design was not imaginary, but true, though not answerable to His Majesty's expectation. Of the quantity I never gave assurance,

nor could. On the other side, if you shall find
that any great number of soldiers be newly sent
to Orinoco, as the cacique of Caliana told us that
they were, and that the passage be re-enforced so
that, without manifest peril of my son, yourself,
and the other captains, you can not pass toward
the mine, then be well advised how you land.
For I know, a few gentlemen excepted, what a
scum of men you have. And I would not for all
the world receive a blow from the Spaniard, to
the dishonor of our nation. I myself, for my
weakness, can not be present. Neither will the
companies land except I stay with the ships, the
galleons of Spain being daily expected."

That part of the fleet detailed for this enterprise set sail for the Orinoco on the 10th of December, and the first of January found Sir Walter
making his head-quarters at Terra de Bri, a port
of Trinidad, about one hundred and fifty miles
north of the mouth of the Orinoco. It took over
three weeks for the fleet to reach the river and
ascend it as far as the island of Taya. A fisher-
man who was on the watch for them carried the

news of their arrival to St. Thomas, a new Spanish town, near the entrance of the Caroni into
the Orinoco. Of the existence of this new St.
Thomas, Raleigh had not been informed, nor was
it to be seen from the river. Passing on, the fleet
arrived at Point Araya on the 1st of January,
1618. The land forces were landed here, intend-
ing to encamp for the night, and the next morning to march in search of the gold mines. A
party of Spaniards, under the command of Ge-
ronimo de Grados, were in ambush on a rising
point between them and the village, and as soon
as night set in surprised the English camp by a
sudden and furious attack. The English rallied,
and, led by young Captain Raleigh and the other
captains, they repelled and drove the Spaniards
back. Presently troops from St. Thomas, under
Diego Palomaque, came to their assistance. Call-
ing upon the pikemen not to wait for the mus-
keteers, Raleigh drove at them, and slew with his
own hand their leader. He was struck by a
musket shot, but, reckless of his wound, he attacked with his sword an officer, named Erinetta,

who defended himself with the butt of his musket, and struck Walter to the ground. Mortally wounded, he cheered on his men, crying, "Go on! May the Lord have mercy on me, and prosper your enterprise!" Erinetta was immediately pierced to the heart by a halbert in the hands of a sergeant. The Spaniards retreat. A party of them took refuge in a monastery at the outskirts of the town. It was stormed and taken. The survivors of the fight escaped to the forest, and finally to the place of refuge occupied by the women and children, who had fled from the town on the approach of the English.

Garcia de Aguilar, who succeeded Palomaque, ordered the women, children, and invalids to be removed to an island in the Orinoco, and organized the defeated troops of St. Thomas. One portion of them was to guard the place of refuge, and another portion to hang about St. Thomas, to prevent the English from holding communication with the Indians, and to cut off any stragglers who might wander from the town.

The death of Walter Raleigh, Jr., threw a

gloom over the English camp, who now occupied the town. He and Captain Cosmar were buried with military ceremonies near the high altar of the Church of St. Thomas.

The same day the vessels of Captain Whitney and Captain Wallaston arrived.

Captain Keymis now took two launches, and ascended the Orinoco in search of the mine; but one of the launches being fired into by an ambuscade of Spaniards near Seiba, and nine out of ten men constituting the crew being shot, he turned back to St. Thomas for re-enforcements. Those that remained in the captured town made inquiries and earnest search for the coveted mines. The Indians whom they met assured them that they existed in this region, but had not been worked for a long time, for want of implements. Although Captain Keymis seems to be disheartened in respect to further efforts to reach the gold mine, George Raleigh was not in the mood to give up, and, taking three boats filled with soldiers and workers, he ascended the Orinoco as far as the mouth of the Guarico, a hundred

leagues or more above St. Thomas.   He was delighted with the country, and saw how attractive
it was to emigration; but he found no gold mines,
nor indeed made any effort to discover them.

When he returned to St. Thomas he found the
company ready to abandon the enterprise.   They
had suffered from sickness, and were in constant
alarm from the hostility of the Spaniards and the
natives.   No one could venture out of the town
without danger of being captured, tortured, and
killed.   One night the town was assaulted by a
large force of the enemy, and fired in several
places.   It was concluded by all parties that the
enterprise was a failure.   The death of young
Raleigh, the sickness of the admiral, over whose
head was suspended the penalty of death, and
the discovery of documents containing the correspondence of the Spanish government at Madrid
with the late governor of Guiana, Palomaque, by
which it appeared that the whole enterprise was
betrayed by King James, even before it left England, all taken with the fact that the Spaniards and
their Indian allies were every-where in force to

resist, disposed Captain Keymis to give up the whole business, and to quit the country. It can not be that he doubted the existence of the precious metals in the interior, for he had in previous voyages satisfied himself of that fact, and had brought off heavy nuggets of gold as samples obtained from the Indians; but he thought it not wise to persist in the face of such obstacles and perils as he encountered, and with symptoms of mutiny in the camp, and with traitors in the rear in the English government. He had sent Sir Walter a letter containing the sad news of his noble son's death, and now he must bear to him the intelligence worse than death or bereavement, of the failure of his long cherished scheme. Taking with them some spoils, six hundred reals in money, a silver basin, some gold nuggets, church bells, and ornaments, the English troops set fire to the town, and embarked in their vessels. Two of the Indian captives they took away with them, one of whom lived to reach England, and to bring back to Guiana the wonderful story of English civilization. Going down the river, he came to

the territory of some Indian tribes, whose caicques
remembered Raleigh, and made flattering offers
to induce the company to settle with them, and
share their wealth, saying that they had held a
portion of the country for Elizabeth; but Keymis
was full of suspicion now of collusion with the
Spaniards, and he declined the overtures. Here
was a chance, some writers think, of redeeming
the expedition from failure, and so thought Raleigh; but it was not to be.

The fleet now made straight for Trinidad,
where they arrived on the 2d of March, 1618,
having been gone less than two months, of which
twenty-five days had been spent at St. Thomas.
The reception which Keymis received from the
admiral may be easily imagined. The death of
young Raleigh had filled the cup of his sorrow to
the brim, and now the report of the defeated expedition and the blasting of his last hope of success
made it to run over. His reproaches were deep
and bitter. The failure to discover the mines would
be ruin to himself and to all concerned. In vain
did Keymis plead that he had not force sufficient

to penetrate into the interior against the combined opposition of Spaniards and Indians; that Gondamar had got ahead of them, and had roused the whole country against the invasion of the English; that if he had persisted and found the mines, it would only be to the final advantage of the Spaniards, for he had not men enough to hold it; that his followers were dispirited upon young Raleigh's death, and he could not rely on them; that he feared Sir Walter himself would sink under his sickness and grief at his son's death, and he did not care "to enrich a company of rascals who made no account of him."

"You have undone me, wounded my credit with the king past recovery," repeated Sir Walter. "You must answer it to the king and to the State." Keymis is overwhelmed with grief and remorse. He retires to his cabin, and writes a long and elaborate apology to the Earl of Arundel, one of the patrons of the enterprise, and brings it to Raleigh for his sanction. But he refused to do so, saying that he had refuted every point, and no satisfactory explanation could be made. "Is that your resolution?" said Keymis. "It is," said Raleigh. "I know then," said Keymis as he withdrew, "what course to take." Not long after a pistol-shot was heard in the cabin over-head. A page was sent to inquire what it meant. The door was shut, and Keymis answered from within that the pistol had long been charged, and he had fired it off. Less than an hour after the lad goes into the room, and finds the captain lying on his bed with the pistol by his side and a knife penetrating his breast. The knife had done what the ball had failed to effect—the veteran seaman was dead.

The whole fleet was now assembled at Trini-dad. During the absence of the exploring expe-dition Sir Walter was in constant expectation of the arrival of a hostile fleet from Spain. The Spaniards at Trinidad had given him considerable annoyance. A boat was fired into at one time by a party in ambush; but no one was killed or wounded. Soon another boat crew wander-ing on shore were attacked, and one man was killed, and a boy was taken captive and never recovered, though Raleigh pursued the enemy and scattered them. The question now arose what course the united fleet should take. Captains Whitney and Wallaston concluded that it would be ruin to return to England, and that something must be done to wreak vengeance on the Spaniards, and to secure spoils to enrich themselves. Raleigh hinted that the Mexican Plate Fleet might be a useful prey. This he said to divert the minds of the captains from undertaking privateering on their own account, for his own mind was fully bent on returning directly homeward; but it was of no avail with Whitney and Wallaston, who took the first opportunity to desert with their ships. It is clear that Raleigh regarded depredations on Spanish commerce as lawful reprisals for the damage done him and his enterprise; but he had promised Arundel and Pembroke to return to England, and he meant to keep his word. His remarks about the Mexican Plate Fleet, however, were quoted against him as proofs that he meant to turn pirate. The news of the taking and burning of St. Thomas had got to Madrid some days before it reached England, and Gondamar had rushed into the presence of King James crying in Spanish, "Pirates! pirates! pirates!" and as James was now bent on a marriage of Prince Charles with the Spanish Infanta, it was proof enough that Walter Raleigh had committed a great crime; and he was glad that he had not pardoned him before he set forth on the expedition, and could now get rid of him by executing the sentence which had been suspended so long.

In a council of the leaders of the expedition it was concluded to pass up the American coast to Newfoundland, and there to repair the ships, and conclude what further to do before returning home. He still clung to the idea of making something out of Guiana. However, at Newfoundland he found his crews so anxious to return to England, and almost ready to mutiny, and some of the ships actually going, that he concluded to follow them, and abandon himself to the mercy of the king. Never was hope more illusive. His doom was already prepared. We next find

him on the Irish coast, and anchoring at Kings-
dale with two or three of his ships, the rest of the
fleet having been scattered by storms.   Thence
Sir Walter proceeds in the *Destiny* to Plymouth,
where he arrived on the 21st of June, 1618.
Captain Pennington's ship was seized by the lord
deputy of Ireland, under orders from the court,
previously given, to attach any and all of the
Guiana squadron which might put into any Irish
port.   Captain Pennington went to London to
seek redress, and was arrested and put in prison.
Such were the first fruits and earnest of what was
in store for Sir Walter.

Chapter XVIII.

ARRESTED ON HIS JOURNEY TO LONDON—EXPEDIENTS TO
ESCAPE—COMMITTED TO THE TOWER—FRUITLESS EF-
FORTS OF QUEEN ANNE IN HIS BEHALF—BROUGHT
BEFORE THE COURT OF THE KING'S BENCH—FORMER
SENTENCE RENEWED AGAINST HIM—HIS EXECUTION
AND BURIAL.

HAVING remained in Plymouth a few weeks,
Sir Walter Raleigh started for London, in
company with his wife and Captain Samuel King,
of the Guiana fleet, a fast friend.   They had proceeded no farther than Ashburton, twenty miles
from Plymouth, when they met Sir Lewis Stukeley, vice-admiral of Devonshire, a relative of Raleigh, who had the king's orders to arrest him,
and to seize his ships.   They turned back immediately to Plymouth, and Stukeley took possession
of the *Destiny*.   He left Sir Walter, with his wife
and servant, at the house of Sir Christopher Harris,

while he busied himself about the affairs of the ship.

There was now a chance for Raleigh to escape. Urged by his wife and friends, he engaged Captain King to hire a vessel to take him to France, and one night two men came and took him in a boat to go to the vessel waiting out in the offing of the harbor. But just before they reached the barge Sir Walter had misgivings as to whether it was honorable for him to take this course, and he ordered the men to turn back. The loving instincts of his wife were in this case wiser than the reasonings of her husband. Under the circumstances, he had a right to protect himself from the injustice and cruelty of the government, as it now began to be manifested by the treatment he and his captains were receiving. It is altogether likely, from the loose manner in which Stukeley guarded him, and from subsequent maneuvers of this officer, that it would not be disagreeable to his employers to have his prisoner escape, and in that way deliver them from the dilemma of disposing of him, so as to satisfy the

vindictiveness of the Spanish court. The statement that, after the death of Raleigh, was made
by the king, called the Declaration, and drawn
up at the instance of Lord Francis Bacon, to jus-
tify the conduct of the king, was false in the
assertion that Raleigh attempted to escape before
the time of his arrest by Stukeley. He thought
of no such thing before it appeared that his life
was in danger.

Soon a peremptory order to Stukeley came
from the council to bring his prisoner to London. They were now accompanied by one
Manourie, a French doctor, employed by Stukeley on pretense of Raleigh's health requiring
medical advice, but really for the purpose of setting a spy over him. To him Raleigh and Captain King talked freely about their affairs. "I
wish," said King, one day, "we were all safe at
Paris." As they passed by his former estate at
Sherbourne, Raleigh remarked to Manourie, "All
this was mine, and it was taken from me unjustly."
These and other talks were reported by Manourie
to Stukeley.

Descending the hill at Wilton, toward Salisbury, Raleigh dismounted and walked with the Frenchman, and opened to him a project which occupied his thoughts, to delay his journey at the latter place until the king, who was expected there in a "progress" over the country, should arrive. His object was to get time to put in writing a full explanation of the Guiana voyage, for his defense with the council, and for his vindication with posterity. The scheme suggested to the doctor was that he should give him some medicine which should make him ill for a time, and dispose Sir Lewis Stukeley to delay the journey. "I shall thus," Manourie reported Raleigh's remarks, "gain time to reach my friends and order my affairs, perhaps even to pacify his majesty. Otherwise, as soon as ever I come to London, they will have me in the Tower, and cut off my head. I can not escape it without counterfeiting sickness, which your vomits will effect without suspicion." This being arranged, as Sir Walter was proceeding to his chamber at Salisbury, he stumbled in the corridor and fell against

238   Sir Walter Raleigh.

a pillar. The plot took; the prisoner was de-
tained; Lady Raleigh, who was in the secret,
and her attendants went on to her house in London; and Captain King was directed to hire a
ship at London or Gravesend, that should be in
readiness at Tilbury, on the Thames, for another
attempt to escape to France. The next morning
a servant came rushing into Stukeley's room,
crying out: "My master is out of his wits. I
have just found him in his shirt, on all fours,
gnawing at the rushes on the boards!"

The doctor was sent to him, and administered
an emetic. He also besmeared his forehead,
arms, and breast with an ointment which brought
out on the skin purple pustules, like the leprosy.
The Bishop of Ely, who was in town and heard
of the case, sent the best of the physicians of
Salisbury to his relief; and these physicians
joined with Manourie in a certificate that it
would not be safe for the prisoner to continue his
journey for some days. Raleigh's object was
gained; he had time to write "The Apology for
the Voyage to Guiana." In less than a week the

king and his court came to Salisbury, and Stukeley received peremptory orders to take his prisoner to London.

On the 7th of August Raleigh arrived at his
house in Broad Street, where, according to orders
previously given, Stukeley was to keep guard
over him instead of taking him to the Tower.
Here he was visited by two emissaries of the
French government, Le Clerc and De Novion,
who made him an offer of a bark to carry him to
Calais.   This the government found out, and
though they were satisfied that Raleigh was pas-
sive in the matter, it complicated his case, and
made it worse.   Captain King came and informed
him that a ketch had been provided, and was
waiting at Tilbury under the command of one
Hart, formerly a boatswain of Captain King.
Stukeley was informed of all this; but he pretended to favor it, having been promised by Raleigh large rewards for his connivance.   He accompanied Raleigh, with his son, Captain King,
and a page to the river's side, where two wher-
ries waited to row the company to the ketch.

They had scarcely got out on the river before they perceived that they were followed by a boat full of men. It was Herbert, a relation of Stukeley, who had been engaged by him for the purpose of apprehending Raleigh when he should have gone so far as to prove that he intended to escape to France. King and Raleigh expressed their suspicions; but Stukeley tried to allay them. Their talk alarmed the watermen, and they slackened their speed. The tide was getting unfavorable, and the ketch could not be reached before daylight, and it was clear that their pursuers would overtake them. In this predicament it was decided to turn back, and when they turned, the suspicious boat turned also, and followed them to Greenwich. Arrived there, Stukeley threw off his disguise, and arrested both Raleigh and King in the name of King James. "Sir Lewis," said Raleigh, "these actions will not turn out to your credit." He was conducted to the Tower, where he parted with his faithful friend, who was allowed to go at liberty.

Le Clerc, who was resident minister of France,

was called to attend at a meeting of the privy council, and explain his visit to Sir Walter. He denied that he had made any overtures to Sir Walter Raleigh to assist him to escape to France, and persisted in denying it even after he was confronted with De Novion, who had confessed it all. It was decreed that Le Clerc should retire to his house, and forbear any further actions as a public minister. This proceeding excited great indignation at the French court. They denied that a man who had been appointed admiral of a fleet of fourteen ships could be pronounced "a traitor," and they asserted that whatever Le Clerc had done, it was not to do King James any "disservice," but only to draw service for him against the Spaniards. For their part of this mean tragedy, Manourie received twenty pounds, and Stukeley nine hundred and sixty-five pounds, three shillings, and sixpence—a poor fee for a treachery which gave him the name of Sir Judas Stukeley.

The doom of Raleigh was now certain to every body. King James had him now wholly in his power, and it was only a question whether he should give him up to Spain to be hanged by them as a buccaneer, or to be brought to the block in England in execution of the sentence before pronounced upon him. He was repeatedly brought before a committee of the privy council for examination. Attorney-general Yelverton charged him with having deceived the king by pretending to have discovered a gold mine which no person knew but himself, and yet he took no miners, nor tools for the business, and gave no orders to his men to search for it. The solicitor-general charged him with abandoning his forces in Guiana, and with "vile and dishonorable speeches full of contumely to the king" since his return to England. Sir Walter replied to all these allegations, and concluded by denying that the Spaniards had any rightful dominion over that region where they had built the new town of St. Thomas. Being charged with proposing to capture the Mexican fleet, he admitted that he talked about taking it, but it was "in order to keep the fleet together."

Not satisfied with what was gained by these examinations, the government appointed Sir Thomas Wilson to have the keeping and oversight of Sir Walter in the Tower, with a view to get from him statements and expressions which might tend his conviction of treason or piracy; but, though he promised that "if he would discover what he knew, the king would forgive him and do him all favor," yet nothing was extracted from Raleigh to his disadvantage. He persisted in defending the whole enterprise as lawful and expedient, and emphatically denied the claims set up by Spain to the exclusive possession of Guiana.

Lady Raleigh was made a prisoner in her own house, under the charge of a Mr. Wallaston, a London merchant, and her furniture and household goods were put under lock and key. The letters which passed between her and her husband were intercepted by Wilson to find accusations against him. A copy of one of Sir Walter's letters to his wife has been preserved, which shows that Wilson and his son Edward had played well the part of a spy. It concludes thus:

"I am sycke and weak. This honest gentleman, Mr. Edward Wilson, is my keeper, and takes much payne with me. My swolne syde keeps me in perpetual pain and unrest. God comfort us.   Yours,   W. R."

Lady Raleigh's reply to Sir Walter's letter was the following:

"I am sory to hear amongst many discomforts that your health is so ill. 'T is meerly sorrow and greaf that with wynde hath gathered into your syde. I hope your health and comforts will mend, and mend us for God. I am glad to hear you have the company and comfort of so good a keeper. I was somewhat dismayed at the first that you had no servant of your own left you; but I hear this night servants are very neces- sary. God requite his courtesyes, and God in mercy look on us.   Yours,

"E. RALEIGH."

Raleigh wrote a letter to the king; also, to his favorite minister, the Marquis, afterward Duke, of Buckingham, to intercede in his behalf. He also appealed to the queen in the following lines, which were among the last verses with which he relieved the tedium and gloom of imprisonment. The queen never ceased to love and respect Raleigh, especially since the death of her first-born son, Prince Henry. Her own health was now failing, and she was in a mood to give earnest heed to the plea of one whose life was suspended by a hair.

"Oh, had Truth power the guiltless could not fall,
Malice win glory, or Revenge triumph;
But Truth alone can not encounter all.

Mercy is fled to God which Mercy made;
Compassion dead; Faith turned to Policy.
Friends know not those who sit in sorrow's shade.

For what we sometimes were we are no more;
Fortune hath changed the shape, and Destiny
Defaced the very form we had before.

All love, and all desert of former times,
Malice hath covered from my sovereign's eyes,
And largely laid abroad supposed crimes.

But kings care not to mind what vassals were,
But know them now as Envy hath described them:
So can I look on no side from Despair.

Cold walls, to you I speak; but you are senseless.
Celestial powers, you hear, but have determined,
And shall determine, to my greatest happiness.

Then unto whom shall I unfold my wrongs,
Cast down my tears, or hold up folded hands?
To her to whom remorse doth most belong.

To her who is the first, and may alone
Be justly called the empress of the Britons.
Who shall have mercy if a queen hath none?

Save those who would have died for your defense;
Save him whose thoughts no treason ever tainted.
For, lo! destruction is not recompense.

If I have sold my duty, sold my faith
To strangers, which was only due to one,
Nothing I should esteem so dear as death.

But if both God and Time shall make you know
That I, your humblest vassal, am opprest,
Then cast your eyes on undeserved woe,

That I and mine may never mourn the miss
Of her we had; but praise our living queen,
Who brings us equal, if not greater, bliss."

Queen Anne immediately addressed a letter in a familiar and earnest style to Buckingham, a copy of which is preserved.

"ANNA R. :

"*My kind dogge*,—If I have any power or credit with you, I pray you let me have a trial of it at this time in dealing sincerely and earnestly with the king that Sir Walter Raleigh's life may not be called in question.

"If you do it so that the success answer my expectation, assure yourself that I will take it extraordinarily kindly at your hands; and rest one that wishes you well, and desires you to continew still, as you have been, a true servant of your master.

"*To the* MARQUIS OF BUCKINGAME."

Buckingham's influence with the king in behalf of Raleigh was forestalled by his devotion to to the project of King James to wed Prince Charles to the Infanta of Spain, and Gondamar had impressed him with the necessity of putting Raleigh out of the way, if the favor of the King of Spain was to be secured. The probability is that he did nothing to gratify the queen in this matter, and save her friend.

The king was informed that the Spaniards preferred not to have the prisoner delivered over to them for execution, but to have him executed in England. In this predicament, Lord Bacon was applied to for counsel as to the legal form of

accomplishing this purpose.   On consultation with
his colleagues, the lord chancellor informed the king
that a person already "attainted of high treason
can not be drawn in question judicially for any
crime since committed;" that the king might give
warrant for Raleigh's execution upon the former
conviction.   At the same time Bacon inconsist-
ently suggested that Raleigh might be called
before the council of state and the judges, on the
charge of "acts of hostility, depredations, and
abuse."   In that case Raleigh could not plead
that he had been pardoned.   The king saw the
contradiction in these advices of his sycophantic
lord chancellor, and preferred the more direct
course of executing the sentence which had been
suspended since 1603.

Accordingly, Raleigh was summoned before
the court of the king's bench.   It was a surprise
to him, and he arose from his bed, where he had
lain suffering from the ague, and, without much
attention to his personal appearance, hurried from
the Tower, followed by one of his old servants.
The servant observed his deshabille, and suggested

to him that he had not combed his head. Sir
Walter naively remarked, in the Devonshire dialect he was accustomed to use with common
people: "Let them kem it that are to have it."
He then added, smiling, "Dost thou know,
Peter, of any plaster that will set a man's head
on again, when it is off?"

At the court the attorney-general produced the
record of conviction, and demanded in the king's
name that the sentence should be executed without delay. The chief-justice then asked the prisoner if he had any thing to say. Raleigh, apol-
gizing for the weakness of his voice on account
of the ague, made reply:

"All I can say, my lord, is this: The judgment I received to die so long since can not now,
I hope, be strained; for since it was his majesty's
pleasure to grant me a commission to proceed on
a voyage beyond the seas, wherein I had martial
power on the life and death of others, so, under
favor, I presume I stand discharged of that judgment. By that commission I gained new life and
vigor; for he that hath power over the life of

others must surely be master of his own. Under
my commission I undertook a voyage, to do
honor to my sovereign, and to enrich his kingdom with gold, of the ore whereof this hand
hath found and taken in Guiana. But the enterprise, notwithstanding my endeavors, hath no
other issue than which was fatal to me—the loss
of my son, and the wasting of my whole estate."

The chief-justice, Montague, here interposed,
saying:

"Treason is a crime which must be pardoned
by express words, not by implication."

"If that be your lordship's opinion," said Raleigh, "I can only put myself upon the mercy
of the king. His majesty, as well as all others
who are here present, have been of opinion that
in my former trial I received but hard measure.
Had the king not been exasperated anew against
me, certain I am that I might have lived a thousand years before he would have taken advantage
of this conviction."

The chief-justice remarked that he had a fair
trial, and he should confess that his former judg-

ment should justly be executed. For fifteen years he had been dead in law, and might at any moment have been cut off. "I know," continued the chief-justice. "you have been valiant and wise, and I doubt not but you retain both these virtues, for now you shall have occasion to use them. Your faith hath heretofore been questioned; but I am resolved that you are a good Christian, for your book, which is an admirable work, doth testify as much." Having added a few words more, expressing his sorrow for his fate, the chief-justice declared that "the execution was granted."

"My lords," said Raleigh, "I desire this much favor, that I may not be cut off suddenly, but may have some time granted me before my execution to settle my affairs and my mind more than they yet are. I have something to do in discharge of my conscience, and I have somewhat to satisfy His Majesty in. I would beseech the favor of pen, ink, and paper. . . . I would beseech your lordships that, when I come to die, I may have leave to speak freely at my farewell.

And here I take God, before whom I shall shortly appear, to be my judge, that I was never disloyal to His Majesty, which I shall testify when I shall not fear the face of any king on earth. And I beseech you all to pray for me."

The king was purposely absent from London, but the royal warrant for execution was now produced, it having been prepared by anticipation. The sentence of hanging was changed to beheading; the time, the following morning.

Raleigh was now taken to the gate-house of Westminster, one story of which was now used for a prison. Here he was visited by friends.

As Raleigh passed from the Hall to the gate-house, he met an old friend, Sir Hugh Barton, and asked him:

"You will come to-morrow morning?"

"Certainly," said Sir Hugh.

"But I do not know what you may do for a place. For my own part, I am sure of one. You must make what shift you can."

So cheerful was the condemned, but innocent, man, that his friends wondered at it, and one said to him, "Do not carry it with too much bravery; your enemies will take exceptions, if you do." "It is my last mirth in this world," he replied. "Do not grudge it to me. When I come to the sad parting, you will see me grave enough." To another friend he said, "The world is but a large prison, out of which some are daily selected for execution."

The Dean of Westminster, Dr. Robert Towson, afterward Bishop of Salisbury, who was appointed to attend him, was impressed by his wonderful buoyancy of spirits and fearlessness of death, and cautioned him in respect to its source. "He was the most fearless of death ever known," wrote the dean, afterward, "and the most resolute and confident, yet with reverence and conscience."

The saddest scene of all was the final interview, at midnight, of Raleigh with his beloved wife. It is best described by his eloquent biographer, Edward Edwards:

"She had buoyed herself with hope till almost the moment of the final meeting in the gate-house. But before she went, some friends broke to her the news, and told her that the lords of council, though they had refused intercession with the king for her husband's life, would empower her to bury him. It was then late on Thursday. It had yet to be told her that early on Friday morning she would be a widow. But the clownish brutality native to James became an unmeant mercy. During that brief space of time Raleigh's thoughts were much bent upon the final vindication of his fame before the world. Into that channel he forced himself to turn his wife's thoughts also. And her love was stronger than her grief. He told her that he could not trust himself to talk about their dear little Carew. Thoughts concerning him must be left unspoken. Speech would but make the parting too hard for both of them. As they were conversing together about Lady Raleigh's task in the event of her husband's misgivings being realized by the forcible prevention of his intended address from the scaffold, the abbey clock told them it was already midnight. She knew that it would be an act of wifely love now to leave him alone, and she com

pelled herself to go.   Her last words were to
tell him of the message about the disposal of his
body.   Then the passionate anguish would no
longer let itself be restrained.   But the loving
purpose of departure was firmly kept.   'It is
well, dear Bess,' said Sir Walter with a parting
smile, 'that thou mayst dispose of that dead
which thou hadst not always the disposing of
when alive.'"

Left alone, Sir Walter spent his time in sup-
plementing his last will and testament, and ap-
pending to it the substance of his replies to the
accusations of Ferne, Stukeley, and Manourie.

Early in the morning he received the com-
munion from Dr. Towson, who testified that he
seemed "very cheerful and merry," and full of
hope that he should satisfy every one of his innocence of the late charges by his final declaration
on the scaffold.   He took his breakfast as usual,
and smoked his pipe, saying to all his attendants
that death seemed to him nothing more than
going on a journey.   He dressed himself in his
usual precise manner, and with special reference

to the mode of his execution. A cup of wine was brought to him just before he left the gate-house. He was asked if it were to his liking. "I will answer you," said he, "as did the fellow who drank of St. Giles's bowl as he went to Tyburn, 'It is a good drink, if a man might but tarry by it.'"

Attended by the dean of Westminster, he followed two sheriffs to the scaffold in the old palace yard near the Parliament House. He bowed to the crowd of persons present, among whom he saw several of his distinguished friends. Noticing a venerable, bald-headed old man standing near, he took from under his hat a night-cap of cut lace, and threw it to him, saying, "You need this, my friend, more than I do."

He ascended the scaffold with a cheerful countenance, but with the air of one whose body was enfeebled by sickness, and out of breath by pushing through the crowd. In that crowd he was pleased to see numbers of the most distinguished commoners and noblemen of the realm standing or sitting on horseback.

Sentence being proclaimed, Sir Walter began his farewell speech, for which he had been so anxious to have the opportunity of delivering. He found it difficult to raise his voice to a pitch sufficient to be heard by the whole assembly, and particularly by his friends, the Earls of Arundel, Oxford, and Northampton, who stood in the balcony. "I have had fits of ague for these two days," he said; "if, therefore, you perceive any weakness in me, ascribe it to my sickness rather than to myself. I am infinitely bound to God that he hath vouchsafed me to die in the sight of so noble an assembly, and not in darkness in that Tower, where I have suffered so much adversity and a long sickness. I thank God that my fever hath not taken me at this time, as I prayed to God it might not."

He then devoted his attention to the noblemen in the balcony, and said that he was afraid he could not make himself heard by them. Whereupon they said, "We will come down to you." He sat down while they were making their way to him. They came directly to where he sat, and

17

shook hands with him heartily and long.   He
then arose, and said:

"There are two main points which, as I con-
ceive, have hastened my coming thither, of which
his majesty hath been informed against me.   The
first, that I had some practice with France.   And
the reason which his majesty had so to believe
was, first, for that when I came to Plymouth, I
had a desire in a small bark to have passed to
Rochelle, and after, because the French agent
came to my house here in London.   But as ever
I hope to see God or to have any benefit or comfort by the passion of my Savior, I never had any
practice with the French king or his embassador
or agent; neither had I any intelligence from
thence; neither did I ever see the French king's
hand or seal as some report [asserting that], I
had a commission from him at sea; neither, as I
have a soul to save, did I know of the French
agent's coming to my house till I saw him in my
gallery.   It is not now a time either to fear or
fla 'er kings.   I am now the subject of death, and
the great God of heaven is my sovereign, before

whose tribunal-seat I am shortly to appear. And, therefore, have a charitable conceit of me. To swear [falsely] is an offense; to swear falsely at any time is a great sin. So to call God to witness an untruth is a sin above measure sinful. But to do it at the hour of one's death, in the presence of Almighty God, before whom one is forthwith to appear, were the greatest madness and sin that could be possible.

"The other matter alleged against me," continued Raleigh, "is that I should have spoken some disloyal, dishonest, and dishonorable words of the king. Mine accuser is a runagate Frenchman, who, having run over the face of the earth, hath no abiding-place. This fellow, because he had a merry wit, and some small skill in chemical medicine, I entertained rather for his taste than his judgment. He perjured himself at Salisbury, revealing that, the next day, the contrary of which he vowed to me the day before. But by the same protestation I have already made, and as I hope for my inheritance in heaven, I did never speak any disloyal, dishonorable, or dishonest

words of the king. If I did, the Lord blot me
out of the book of life. Nay, I will protest further that I never thought such evil of him in my
heart; and therefore it seemeth somewhat strange
that such a base fellow should receive credit.
Touching Sir Lewis Stukeley, he is my country-
man and kinsman, and I have this morning taken
the sacrament with Master Dean, and I have for-
given both Stukeley and the Frenchman. Yet thus
much, I think, I am bound in charity to speak
of it, that others may take warning how they
trust such men. Sir Lewis Stukeley hath testified
before the lords that I told him my Lord Carew
sent me word to get me gone, when I first landed.
I protest, upon my salvation, neither did my Lord
Carew send me any such word, neither did I tell
Stukeley any such matter. He accused me, again,
that I should tell him that my Lord Carew and
my Lord Doncaster would meet me in France,
which was never my speech nor my thought.
Thirdly, he accused me that I showed him, in a
letter, that I would give him ten thousand pounds
for my escape. I never made him offer of ten

thousand pounds, or one thousand pounds.   If I
had had half so much, I could have done better
with it.   I did show him in a letter that if he
would go with me his debts should be paid when
he was gone.   For, as to my seeking escape, I
can not deny it.   I had advertisement that it
would go hard with me.   I desired to save my
life.   And as for that I did feign myself sick at
Salisbury, and by art made my body full of blis-
ters, to put off the time of coming before the
council, I hope it was no sin.   The prophet
David, a man after God's own heart, did feign
himself mad, and let the spittle fall down on his
beard.   I find not that recorded as a fault in
David, and I hope God will never lay it to my
charge.   I hoped by delay to gain time for obtaining my pardon.

"But Sir Lewis Stukeley did me a further
injury, which I am very sensible of, howsoever it
seem not to concern myself.   In my going up to
London, we lodged at Sir Edward Parham's
house.   He is an ancient friend and follower of
mine, whose lady is my cousin-german.   There

Stukeley made it to be suggested unto me, and himself told me, he thought I had some poison given me. I know it grieves the gentleman there should be such a conceit held. And as for the cook who was suspected, having been once my servant, I know he would go a thousand miles to do me good.

"For my going to Guiana, many thought I never intended it, but intended to gain my liberty,—which I would I had been so wise as to have kept. But, as I shall answer it before the same God before whom I am shortly to appear, I endeavored, and I hoped, to have enriched the king, myself, and my partners. But I was undone by Keymis, a willful fellow, who, seeing my son slain, and myself unpardoned, would not open the mine, and killed himself.

"It was also told the king that I was brought by force to England, and that I did not intend to come back again. I protest that when the voyage succeeded not, and that I resolved to come home, my company mutinied against me. They fortified the gun-room against me, and kept me within my own cabin; and would not be satisfied except I would take a corporal oath not to bring them into England until I had gotten the pardons of four of them,—there being four men unpardoned. So I took that oath. And we came into Ireland, where they would have landed in the north parts. But I would not, because there the inhabitants were all Redshanks. So we came to the South, hoping from thence to write to his majesty for their pardons. In the mean time I offered to send them to places in Devon or Cornwall, to lie safe till they had been pardoned.

"I am glad that my Lord of Arundel is here; for, when I came down to my ship, his lordship and divers others were with me. At the parting salutation, his lordship took me aside, and desired me freely and faithfully to resolve to him one request, which was, whether I made a good voyage or bad, yet I should return again into England. I made you," turning to Lord Arundel, who was on the scaffold, "a promise, and gave you my faith, that I would."

Lord Arundel responded: "And so you did.

It is true that they were were the last words I
spake unto you."

After a few desultory remarks on various un-
important matters, Sir Walter concluded:

"I will yet borrow a little time of Master
Sheriffs, to speak of one thing more. It doth
make my heart bleed to hear such an imputation
laid upon me. It was said that I was a perse-
cutor of my Lord of Essex, and that I stood in a
window over against him when he suffered, and
puffed out tobacco in disdain of him. I take my
God to witness that my eyes shed tears for him
when he died. And, as I hope to look in the
face of God hereafter, my Lord of Essex did not
see my face when he suffered. I was far off in
the Armory when I saw him, but he saw not me.
And now my soul hath been many times grieved
that I was not near with him when he died, because I have understood that he asked for me at
his death, to be reconciled to me. I confess I
was of a contrary faction. But I knew that my
Lord of Essex was a noble gentleman, and that
it would be worse with me when he was gone;

for those that did set me up against him did afterward set themselves against me."

He closed with an earnest prayer for the
divine mercy and blessing.

He then asked the people present to pray
for him:

"And now I entreat you all to join with me
in prayer to the Great God of Heaven, whom I
have grievously offended. I have many, many
sins for which to beseech God's pardon. Of a
long time my course was a course of vanity. I
have been a seafaring man, a soldier, and a
courtier, and the temptations of the least of
these overthrow a good mind and a good man.
I die in the faith as professed by the Church of
England. I hope to be saved and have my sins
washed away by the precious blood and merits
of our Savior, Christ."

Proclamation was now made for all persons to
leave the scaffold. Sir Walter then threw off his
cloak. His hat and some money he gave to his
attendants. He then bade farewell to his friends
around him. He asked Lord Arundel to entreat

the king to allow no calumnious publications
against his character when he was gone.

"I have a long journey to go," he said, "and
must therefore speedily take my leave." Taking
off his gown and doublet, he presented himself as
ready to the executioner.

He then asked to see the ax. The executioner, bewildered, hesitated, until he asked the
second time. He felt the blade to test its sharp-
ness, and kissed it, saying, "This gives me no
fear. It is a sharp and fair medicine to cure me
of all my diseases." He then said, "When I
stretch forth my hands, dispatch me."

He then saluted the assembly around him, and
said, "Give me your prayers." He then kneeled
for the last prayer.

The executioner asked which way he would
have his head directed. He answered, "If the
heart be right, it were no matter which way the
head was laid." The executioner turned his face
to the east as he laid his head upon the block,
and threw over his body his cloak. In a moment
the hand was raised, as a signal for the stroke.

But the man trembled and hesitated. "What dost thou fear?" cried Sir Walter. "Strike, man, strike." The ax fell twice, and the head dropped upon the stage, and all was over.

The head was lifted, shown to the crowd, and then deposited in a red leather bag. That and the body, enveloped in Sir Walter's cloak, were conveyed in a coach to the house of Lady Raleigh. By her the head was embalmed, and kept in a case while she lived, and then left to her son Carew, who at his death requested that it should be buried in the same grave with himself.

The body was interred in the chancel of St. Margaret's Church in Westminster. There now the traveler will read on a tablet of brass, replacing in 1845 one of wood, this inscription probably copied from the original:

"Within the chancel of this church was interred
the body of the great SIR WALTER RALEIGH,
on the day he was beheaded in Old Palace
Yard, Westminster, October 29, 1618.
Reader, should you reflect on his errors, remember his many virtues, and that he was a
mortal."

In his Bible at the gate-house these truthful and touching lines were found:

> "Even such is time that takes on trust
> Our youth, our joys, our all we have,
> And pays us but with age and dust;
> Who in the dark and silent grave,
> When we have wandered all our ways,
> Shuts up the story of our days!
> But from this earth, this grave, this dust,
> The Lord shall raise me up, I trust."

The popular sympathy with Raleigh was manifested by the promiscuous crowd that came to the execution. In that assembly were Sir John Eliot and John Hampden, whose resistance to the arbitrary acts of Charles I has made them immortal. From that hour the writings of Raleigh were text-books to the English patriots, who sought to limit the prerogatives of the crown, and to enlarge the liberties of the subject.

The sad story of Raleigh's fate was the topic of conversation in every circle in England, and in every court in Europe. At St. Paul's Church, where noblemen, merchants, and professional men were wont to congregate twice a day for conver-

sation and business communication, a leading
merchant of London, Mr. Edward Weimark,
speaking of the Secretary of State, Sir Robert
Naunton, said he wished that Sir Walter Raleigh's
head were on his shoulders. This remark was
reported to the privy council, and Weimark was
called to account for it. He admitted the remark, but said it only meant that two heads
were better than one. Not long after subscrip-
tions were taken at the council chamber for St.
Paul's Cathedral, and Weimark subscribed one
hundred pounds; but on the Secretary's remark-
ing significantly that two hundred were better
than one, he thought it prudent for him to double
his subscription.

The enemies of Raleigh were obnoxious to the
popular dislike. Manourie was treated with contempt, and Sir Lewis Stukeley was repelled from
respectable society. One day his office as vice-
admiral of Devon brought him to the house of
Lord Charles Howard. He was met by the earl
with an outburst of indignation. "Darest thou
to come into my presence, thou base fellow, who

art reputed the common scorn and contempt of all men? Were it not in my own house, I would cudgel thee with my staff for presuming to speak to me." Stukeley complained to the king of this treatment. "What should I do with him?" said James. "Hang him? On my sawle, mon, if I hang all that spoke ill of thee, all the trees in the island were too few." Not a year had elapsed before Stukeley was detected in debasing the king's coin in the Whitehall Palace, and was condemned to be hung. The sentence was commuted for confiscation of most his possessions. He then took refuge at his country-seat in Affton; but being every-where scorned by poor and rich, his life was a burden, and he fled to the little island of Lundy, sixteen miles off the coast of Devon, and there, in less than two years, in the old ruined "Moresco Castle," he died, a wretched, heart-broken man.

The king found it necessary by the prostituted but plausible pen of Bacon to publish an apology for his treatment of Raleigh, entitled, "A Declaration of the Demeanor and Carriage of Sir Walter Raleigh," in which are some palpable contradictions and perversions of the facts in the case. The curse of God rested upon that mean and cowardly king, and upon his family, culminating in the beheading of Charles I, and the final extinction of the royal house of the Stuarts.

Lady Raleigh survived her noble husband twenty-nine years. Her son Carew, who was thirteen years of age at his father's death, vindicated the characier of his father in a treatise, entitled, "*Brief Relations of Sir Walter Raleigh's Troubles.*" He was highly educated, and possessed of more than ordinary literary genius. He failed to recover his father's forfeited estate of Sherbourne, but became possessed of an ample fortune by marriage. At his death he requested to be buried in his father's grave.

THE END.

BOOKS FOR THE JUNIORS.

Here are **Three Choice Libraries,** put up in neat boxes, just right for the Junior League, the Primary Class in the Sunday-school, or the Little Folks at Home.

WINDSOR GEMS. Ten Volumes.

Little Henry.
The Story of a Cuckoo Clock.
Katie's Christmas Lesson.
The Witch of the Quarryhut.
Tom's Memorable Christmas.

The Little Forester.
Our Father.
The White Dove.
The Bracelets.
Waste Not, Want Not.

Each volume is 4¼x6¼ inches in size, and contains 64 pages. Bound in cloth, handsomely illuminated. Text by Annie S. Swan, Miss Edgeworth, and others. Illustrated. Price, post-paid, $2.00.

RUGBY GEMS. Twelve Volumes.

Little Blue Mantle.
Nannette's New Shoes.
Little Golden Locks.
Ways of Wisdom.
Syd's New Pony.
Paul Cuffee.

Bess.
Captain John's Adventures.
The Little Woodman.
The Orphan of Kinloch.
Blanche Gamond.
The Pearl Necklace.

Each volume 4¼x6¼ inches in size, and contains 64 pages. Illuminated cloth binding. Text by Annie S. Swan, Robina F. Hardy, and others. Illustrated. Price, post-paid, $2.40.

THE TINY LIBRARY. Twelve Volumes.

Harry Carlton's Holiday.
The Peddler's Loan.
What a Little Cripple Did.
Bobby.
Matty and Tom.
Little Chrissie, and Other Stories.

The Broken Window.
A Little Loss and a Big Find.
Letty Young's Trial.
Brave Boys.
Little Jem, the Rag Merchant.
John Madge's Cure for Selfishness.

Each volume is 3½x4¼ inches in size, and contains 64 pages. Illuminated cloth binding. Beautiful stories for younger children. Illustrated. Price, post-paid, $1.80.

CURTS & JENNINGS, Cincinnati, Chicago, St. Louis.

JOY THE DEACONESS.

By ELIZABETH E. HOLDING.

12mo. Cloth. Illustrated. 213 pages, ... 90 cents.

"You think people ought to help other people who are in trouble? You said you thought Christians ought to do all they could for the Lord. It was just those wretchedly poor people the Savior cared so much about. He could n't bear to see people suffering with no one to help them."

"In this book the gifted author tells an intensely interesting story which illustrates many phases of the life of both nurse and visiting deaconesses. It gives an immense amount of information."—MRS. LUCY RIDER MEYER, in *The Message.*

THE LATTER-DAY EDEN.

By HENRY TUCKLEY.

12mo. Cloth. 251 pages, ... 90 cents.

"The importance of making the home happy is shown from the fact that, if we are not happy in our family and domestic relations, we can not know real happiness in any relation or in any sphere. Take this key out of the arch, and down topples the bridge; and it is beyond a question that the keystone of earthly bliss is household bliss."

"The author rightly appreciates the very great importance of the home as the foundation of our social economy and the nursery of heaven. He has written plainly and wisely to husbands and wives, to fathers and mothers, to children as such, and to children as brothers and sisters of one family. . . . His attitude is not pedantic, nor is it dogmatic, but helpful in a plain-spoken, easily comprehended way."—*Interior.*

CURTS & JENNINGS, Cincinnati, Chicago, St. Louis.